JEZEBEL'S REDEMPTION

JACQUELIN THOMAS

Jezebel's Redemption © 2018 by Jacquelin Thomas

ISBN: 978-1533558640

All rights reserved.

"But one thing I do: forgetting what lies behind and straining forward to what lies ahead, I press on toward the goal for the prize of the upward call of God in Christ Jesus."

Philippians 3:13-14

Chapter 1

FORTY-THREE YEARS OLD, Jessica Ricks aka Jessica Campana aka Reina Cannon was finally a free woman.

The oppressive June humidity settled over her like a heavy coat, but it was better than being behind the high security fence. After eight long years in the Eastern Correctional Institution in Maury, North Carolina, Jessica was grateful that she did not have to spend another day in that place, her 16-year sentence shortened by good behavior and for being an exemplary inmate. She was now free to return to Raleigh, fiancé, Clayton Wallace, and her family.

When the heavy gates closed behind her, Jessica turned to look back at the two-story facility which sat on 38 acres. She didn't look back with a heart filled with despair because it was in this place that she had found herself—found her peace and her purpose.

She ran her fingers through her soft, brown curling tendrils, which flattered her olive-green eye color. Jessica wondered if Clayton would still consider her the same attractive women he once thought her to be. For the past eight years, he'd seen her behind a wall of glass. He had not visited as much as her siblings because Clayton had a phobia of prisons.

She placed a hand over her eyes to ward off the bright sunlight. He should have been here by now.

"Hey you..." someone called out.

Smiling, Jessica turned in time to see her sister, Chrissy St. Paul pull up in a black convertible BMW. "I was expecting Clayton to pick me up."

"His flight was delayed, so he asked me to do it."

Jessie got into the car. "Thanks for coming to get me. Nice look for you."

"This is Aiden's car. He took mine in for mainte-nance. I'm an SUV girl, especially with the kids. Caleb plays basketball and Lenore is a cheerleader. We stay on the go, so we need room for groceries, equipment... everything."

The two sisters embraced.

"You want to go straight home, or would you like to get something to eat?" Chrissy asked as she drove away from the prison.

"Girl, I've been dreaming of seafood for the past week."

"Seafood, it is," Chrissy said.

"I've lost so much weight. I can stand to gain a pound or two."

Chrissy chuckled. "I think you look great. You're well-toned, like you've been doing some weightlifting."

"I did," Jessica stated as she settled into the car. "Where are we going?"

"There's this great seafood restaurant called Sho' Nuff in Durham. You're going to love it."

"Do they have crab legs?"

Chrissy nodded. "And shrimp. I always get the spicy garlic."

Jessica chuckled. "Girl, you making my mouth water just thinking about it." She was thrilled to see her sister. It had taken her some time to get used to the idea that she had a real relationship with her siblings. Despite all she'd done, neither Holt or Chrissy had abandoned her. During her time locked in that cell, they sent care packages, visited, and kept her encouraged. *I don't think I would've made it without the support I received from them and Clayton.*

During the ride, Chrissy talked about her children. "Caleb and Lenore can't wait to see you."

"I can't wait to finally meet them. I'm glad you didn't bring them to the prison. I never wanted them to see me that way."

"All they know is that it's been a while since you lived in Raleigh. Aiden and I shielded them from all the other stuff. You can tell them everything when they're older and can understand."

"Thank you," Jessica said.

"Have you and Clayton discussed a wedding date yet?" Chrissy asked when they were seated at a table near the window an hour and a half later.

"Yes. We're going to have a small ceremony in two

weeks. He's going to give his initial sermon on that Sunday —Clayton wants to be married when he steps up into the pulpit. I'm not sure why, but it works for me. I should've married that man a long time ago."

Chrissy peeled a shrimp. "I guess we have a lot to do in a brief amount of time."

While she ate, she studied her sister's face. Chrissy wore her golden-brown hair in its natural curly state. Her tawny complexion, exotic gray eyes, and heart-shaped face was like Jessie Belle's. Before the cosmetic surgery, Jessica once shared the same color eyes and features as her twin— the only difference was that she had a tiny mole on her lip —like Jessie Belle.

"How do you really feel about my marrying Clayton?" Jessica asked while cracking open a crab leg. The lingering scent of garlic, seafood spices and crabmeat made her mouth water. She could hardly wait to taste the succulent meat.

"I'm happy for you," Chrissy responded. "He's spent some time with me and Aiden while you were away. I really believe that Clayton's a different man. He's been studying the Word with Traynor and he gave a powerful testimony a few weeks back. Traynor seems to really like him... sis, I just want you to be happy."

"I don't ever want to see the inside of a prison as an inmate again," Jessica said. "I'm not going to do anything to send me back there." She wiped her mouth with the edge of her napkin. "I found my purpose, Chrissy. I'm going into the ministry. Clayton and I have talked about it and we both feel the calling on our lives. I felt it when I was younger, but I shrugged it off. I felt like God couldn't use someone like me." She lowered her voice. "I hadn't... hurt... killed anyone, but I wasn't living right."

"I think that's wonderful, Jess." Chrissy wiped her hands, then reached over and covered her sister's hand with her own. "You've changed as well. God can use anyone. Look at me... I was a prostitute and I pushed my own mother over a balcony. I could have easily killed her. The truth is at the time, I wanted her dead. Look at how God has turned things around for me, even in my own mess."

"I know that it's not going to be easy—especially after everything I've done. Every time I'd start to doubt, I think about Paul and how God was able to use him." Jessica picked up another crab cluster.

"Amen."

"I feel terrible about the things I did," Jessica confessed.

"You can't let your past weigh you down, sis. God has forgiven you. Now you have to find a way to forgive yourself." Chrissy sliced into a sausage link with her fork. "I love this place."

Jessica nodded in agreement. "It's number one on my list of favorites places to eat. Thanks for bringing me here." She took several sips of water, then said, "I'm so thankful for you and Holt. You both could've turned your backs on me, but you didn't. Even when I tried to turn y'all away—you refused to leave. Even Traynor stuck by me..."

"We love you."

"I remember a time when you couldn't stand the very sight of me."

Chrissy shrugged dismissively. "It's the past, Jessica. We're both very different people now. Let's learn from our past, live in the present and look forward to the future."

A smile tugged at her lips. "Agreed."

After they finished eating, Chrissy dropped Jessica off at the French country-styled house near North Hills owned by Clayton. He'd relocated to Raleigh when she'd decided to return to the city to seek revenge against Natalia and Mary Ellen. Deep down, Jessica was surprised that he'd stayed in North Carolina while she was incarcerated. But what surprised her more was the relationship Clayton had built with Traynor. He looked to the pastor as a mentor.

A twinge of guilt flashed through her at the thought of Mary Ellen. As far as everyone was concerned, the woman's death was considered an accident. Only she and Clayton knew the truth... God knew the truth as well. Jessica had tried to tell Chrissy once during a visit, but her sister stopped her and told her to keep whatever she was going to say, between her and God. Deep down, she believed Chrissy knew what she was going to confess, but perhaps she thought it might tear apart the family they both so desperately wanted.

"I need to pick up the kids. I'd bring them by, but we have Bible Study tonight," Chrissy was saying. "I'll bring them tomorrow after school. Oh, Holt and Frankie are planning to stop by your place when he gets off from work."

"Great," Jessica said. "I'm going to take a nice bubble bath—something I haven't been able to do for eight years."

Fifteen minutes later, she exhaled a long sigh of contentment as she soaked in the tub.

Satisfaction pursed her mouth. Jessica felt blissfully happy and fully alive for the first time in years.

She felt a warm glow flow through her as she shifted her position. She vowed she would never take anything so simple as a bathtub with hot, bubbly water for granted ever again.

Jessica waited to get out of the tub when the water started to cool. She wrapped herself into a fluffy towel and padded barefoot into her bedroom. She glanced over at the clock on the nightstand. Holt would arrive within the half hour.

She dressed in a pair of leggings and a tee-shirt, then slipped on a pair of flip flops.

Jessica pulled her hair into a ponytail. Eying her reflection, she whispered, "Thank you,

Lord. Thank you for letting me come home."

Humming softly, she went downstairs.

Just as she reached the bottom step, the doorbell rang.

Smiling, Jessica opened the front door.

Holt and Frankie stood there, huge grins on their faces.

"Get in here," she urged, fighting back tears. "I'm so happy to see you both."

Inside the foyer, Jessica hugged Frankie, then Holt. "We can sit in the living room," she told them.

"You look good," Frankie said when they were all seated.

"I feel great. I just had a nice bubble bath. If you too weren't coming over—I'd probably still be in that tub—soaking in that water was so soothing."

"We're so glad you're home."

Jessica met her brother's gaze. "Thanks for saying that, Holt."

"I mean it."

"I believe you," she responded. "How are the children?"

"Great," Frankie said. "Growing like faster than I can handle. They are not my little babies anymore."

"I can't wait to see them." Jessica surveyed her brother's wife. Frankie was tall—around five six, and dark-skinned. She was full-figured and carried her weight well. She wore a bright-colored scarf wrapped around her long dreadlocks. "Your hair has gotten so long. You started your locks right before I went to prison."

"I did, and I love them."

"They look really nice on you."

Holt agreed. "My Nubian Queen still takes my breath away."

Frankie grinned. "Thank you, baby."

"So," Jessica interrupted with a short laugh. "Tell me about my nieces and nephew."

"Holt Jr. will be twelve in December and the twins just turned ten." Holt grew silent for a moment. "I wish Mama and Mary Ellen could be here."

He's still grieving, she thought silently. "I'm so sorry." The words shot out of her mouth before she could stop them.

His gaze met her own. "I need to say this to you, Jessica. I want you to know that I bear no ill will toward you. I forgive you for everything you've done—known and unknown. I know how much you wanted to change, and you've done that. I praise God for the way He's transformed your life. You are my sister, regardless of all that's happened. *I love you*."

He knows. He knows that I had something to do with Mary Ellen's death. Just thinking of how he must be feeling right now, shattered her. Jessica didn't bother to wipe away her tears. "How can you love someone like me? I know that it's the God in you, but... *me*..."

"It wasn't easy," Holt admitted. "Frankie and I had some long talks about my feelings where you were concerned. But once I learned the truth about everything you went through... I guess I could understand how you got to that place of darkness."

"I am not that same person, Holt." It was important to Jessica that he believed her. They had gotten so close while she was in prison, or so she thought.

"I know that," he said. "Because if you were—you would not be in our lives. I would never let my children near you."

Jessica searched anxiously for the meaning behind his words. She felt a momentary panic as her mind jumped to the fact that Holt might hold off from letting her see his children. The thought was a stab in her heart and tore at her insides.

As if Frankie sensed what she might be thinking, she

interjected, "What my husband is saying is that we believe in you, Jessica."

Her stomach clenched tight, she said, "What I believe my brother is saying is that he's giving me a second chance and I'd better not blow it. *Message received.*"

"If you feel threatened or need to talk about anything, I'm here for you," Holt stated. "You don't have to go it alone anymore. You have a circle of people cheering you on."

"I recognized that the day you all showed up after I was arrested... when I had to go to court and while I was locked up. I give you my word—I'm going to continue seeing a therapist and take my medication."

Holt got up and moved to sit beside her. "Sweetheart, I don't think of you as broken—not anymore. But I'm not going to say that I have a hundred percent confidence that you won't be tempted to revert back to some type of negative behavior. That's how the enemy works—he uses our weaknesses against us."

Jessica nodded in agreement. "I know, which is why I know that I have to stay prayed up and in the Word. I've learned what my triggers are, and I've worked on strategies for dealing with them." She was grateful to have this conversation with Holt. Jessica did not want there to be any bad feelings between them, so she wanted to address any concerns he and Frankie might have. She considered that it was easier on them while she was locked behind double security fences. "Look, I don't expect that y'all are going to just up and have all this faith in me. I know that I have to earn your trust and I'm okay with that."

"Frankie and I would like you and Clayton to join us for dinner this evening," Holt said. "The kids can't wait to meet you."

She looked up at him. "Are you sure about this?"

He nodded. "It's time they met Auntie Jessica."

She could barely contain her joy. "Thank you... thank you both." Jessica glanced over at the clock on the fireplace. "Clayton should be boarding right about now. I spoke with him right before I got into my bath."

Frankie was the first to stand up. "Dinner will be ready by seven. We'd better be on our way—I need to pick up some things from the grocery store."

Jessica rose to her feet. "Thank you for everything." She embraced her sister-in-law. She hugged Holt next. "You won't regret giving me this chance."

He smiled. "I believe you. We'll see you at the house."

Jessica escorted them to the door.

Alone, she thought back to her encounter with God—the one that changed her life for the better. It happened one day while she was in her cell. That particular day, it was quiet for a change—the silence almost deafening.

That day, she felt God speak the words, "Go and share." The voice was loud and the tone commanding.

Jessica became overwhelmed with emotion. I couldn't believe that God had spoken to me at all, but even more so at the words I heard. Go and share? Go and share what? But then it hit me when I realized what God was telling me to do.

"Surely You can't mean share my past, Lord. You don't mean for me to go and share what I prefer to keep secret."

But deep down, I knew the answer and I didn't like it. I did not want to talk about all the horrible things I'd done. Sure, I'd gratefully accepted His forgiveness and healing, but I wasn't ready to accept His call to give me a purpose.

That evening at Bible study, the Chaplain talked about a man who lived as an outcast, naked and alone in the tombs near Galilee. He spoke of how the poor man had been tormented with demons. When this man saw Jesus, he fell to his knees and begged for mercy. Jesus commanded the demons to leave this man—they were cast into a herd of pigs. After he was healed, the man was so overwhelmed with gratitude that he wanted to remain by Jesus's side, but Christ had other plans for this man. He told him to go and share his story. The man did as he was told. His past and healing became the foundation of a purpose in life that he never imagined.

That was the night Jessica learned that God never wastes a person's pain. His purpose for her was not despite her past, but because of it.

Chapter 2

AS SOON AS she heard the lock turn, Jessica sprinted to the front door, a grin overtaking her features as she took in his smooth, dark chocolate complexion, the close cropped hair and neat mustache.

Clayton was home.

Tall and muscular, he swept her up in his arms as soon as she flung the door open.

"Put me down..." her laughter echoed through the candlelit foyer as she squirmed in his arms. He'd lifted her as though she were as light as a feather, the warmth of his body flooding through her as her arms looped around his neck instinctively. Her heart raced at being in his arms, even if he were only acting silly.

They smiled at each other a long time, until Clayton quietly commented, "It's good to hear that sweet laugh of yours." He seemed to be peering at her intently, his warm brown gaze intense.

"I haven't had much to laugh about over the years."

"Now we can change that," he remarked, taking a step toward her. Clayton kissed her tenderly. "I've missed you so much, babe."

She stared with longing at him. Jessica wrapped her arms around him, feeling safe. "I've missed this. I hated every moment I was away from you."

He led her toward a round table which held a huge display of fresh flowers so colorful that it was the focal point of the room.

"I noticed you replaced the living room furniture."

His gaze was as soft as a caress. "I thought you might want something new."

"I love the color scheme," Jessica said. "Sage green with touches of lavender and yellow."

"I'm sorry that I wasn't there to pick you up. I sold the beauty supply stores and put the money in an account for you. I want us to start fresh. I had to change my reservation because of some last-minute issues, then the flight kept getting delayed."

"It's fine," she assured him. "You're here now. Chrissy and I had lunch; Holt and Frankie came by. I really enjoyed spending time with them. Oh, they invited us to join them for dinner—if you're not too tired."

"Just let me take a shower and I'll be ready."

"I noticed that you got rid of your reef collection," Jessica said. "What did you do with it?"

"Nikko wanted it," he responded. "I removed anything that could be considered harmful before I gave it to him."

She nodded. "You didn't have to get rid of it, but I do believe that it was the right thing to do."

Taking her hand in his, Clayton said, "I hope you still want to marry me."

Jessica broke into a smile. "Of course, I do."

She allowed him to lead the way upstairs.

While Clayton showered, Jessica searched for something to wear. She was looking forward to seeing her nieces and nephew. Everyone was so welcoming. Traynor had called earlier to say he and Angela were in Tennessee for a convention but would be home on Saturday.

An hour later, they arrived at Holt and Frankie's house.

"Auntie Jessica," Holt Jr. said. "I think I've seen you before. When I was little."

She smiled. "I don't think so, but I'm so very happy to finally meet you and your sisters. I've dreamed of this day for a long time."

"Why didn't you just come to visit?"

"I was away... I couldn't get here until now."

"Uncle Clayton told us that you'd cry when you saw us." He held up a small packet of tissues. "I got this in case you do."

Tears spilled over and ran down her cheeks. "He was r-right... thank you for being so thoughtful."

Holt Jr. embraced her. "I'm glad you're here, Auntie."

"He's been waiting by the door since we told them you and Clayton were coming over," Frankie said in a low whisper.

The twins joined them in the family room.

"Let me see if I can guess who is who," Jessica said. The girls were identical, but she had stared at the photos of them taken over the years long enough to believe that she could tell them apart. She pointed to the little girl on the left. "You're Nadia. So, this has to be Nya."

The girls giggled.

"How could you tell them apart?" Holt Jr. asked. Usually, everybody gets them confused."

"I think it may be a twin thing," Clayton said with a chuckle. "Your Aunt Chrissy and Aunt Jessica are twins."

"We're not identical twins like you two," she interjected. "Your dad told me that Nadia busted her lips when she went to her first skating party. There's a tiny little scar just below her lip. That's how I knew."

Holt joined them a few minutes later, smiling as he watched his children vying for Jessica's attention.

"Dinner's ready," Frankie announced.

They gathered around the dining room table.

"Everything is delicious," Jessica said. "Thank you for having us over."

"I didn't want you to have to worry about cooking on your first night home. I also made some baked ziti for you to take home."

"Frankie, thank you for doing all of this."

"It's my pleasure," she responded with a smile.

"Does Frankie know how much you love baked ziti?" Jessica asked when they returned home.

"No, I never mentioned it. I spent a lot of time with Traynor and I never said anything to him about it—we talked mostly about the Bible and ministry. Never about food."

"I guess you could call it divine intervention," she said with a chuckle. Jessica saw the lustful gleam in his gaze. She'd played this scenario in her mind several times over the years. "Honey, I know it's been a while, but... Clayton, I'd like to wait until our wedding night," she said. "I want to start our marriage off the right way. I know it sounds funny, especially since we used to live together."

"No, I agree with you. We made a vow to the Lord to live right and that's what we're gonna do. Besides, our wedding is only a couple of weeks away. I've waited eight years—I can wait two more weeks."

"I think we should sleep in separate rooms," Jessica suggested, although the prolonged anticipation was almost unbearable. "That way, we won't be tempted."

Clayton laughed. "*You* don't want to be tempted. Afraid you won't be able to control yourself?"

"You're funny," Jessica responded. "I hope you don't mind if I take the master bedroom."

"I don't mind at all." Staring at her with longing, he pulled her closer to him. "I'm glad you're home."

"So am I."

They walked down the hall to the media room.

She settled down on the sofa beside Clayton. "Do you ever hear from Nikko and Miguel?"

"Not much," he said. "I think it's best to distance myself from my old life."

She agreed.

Clayton got up and strode behind the bar in the media

room, opened the cooler and retrieved a bottle of Champagne. He poured the chilled liquid into two glasses. "I want us to have a toast." He handed her the glass, standing close by her side. "To the beginning of a great future, for both of us."

Jessica raised her glass, touching the rim of it to Clayton's before drinking. "To dreams coming true."

Chapter 3

"DEAN, can you believe they let that murdering witch out of prison?" Natalia Anderson uttered as she hung up the telephone. "Jessica is free. She's been out since yesterday."

He picked up the newspaper and scanned the headlines while drinking a cup of coffee. "I've heard that she's made a lot of changes for the better from Traynor."

Sending a sharp look in his direction, Natalia said, "She *killed* my friend and her husband."

His left eyebrow rose a fraction. "Hon, she's on probation. If Jessica does anything wrong—she'll be back behind bars before she can blink."

She folded her arms across her chest. "They never should've let her out in the first place."

His expression was tight with strain. "I hope you are not going to obsess about this woman, Natalia. We have two beautiful children to raise, a law firm to run... we have our lives to live."

She nodded. "I know you're right, but it's just not that

easy for me to just forget all the horrible things she's done. Now that she's back in Raleigh, I'm bound to run into that woman at some point."

"When and if that happens—we will deal with it then."

Natalia could tell from Dean's tone that the discussion had ended.

He just doesn't understand, she thought to herself. *He doesn't know what it's like to have someone try to kill you. Jessica should still be incarcerated. She's dangerous.* Frustrated, she navigated to the kitchen to check on dinner.

"Minx... Daniel... it's time to wash your hands. The food will be ready in a few minutes."

Seven-year-old Daniel was the first one seated at the table. Four-year-old Minx joined her brother with their father in tow.

"I made spaghetti," she announced brightly.

"Yea..." the children said in unison.

"I love sketti," Minx added.

"It's your daddy's favorite as well."

They exchanged a polite, simultaneous smile.

Natalia and Dean decided that they would never argue in front of their children, so they pretended the tension impregnating the air did not exist. She listened to her daughter's constant chatter and laughed. She loved being a mother and a wife.

She found her husband in his office later,

"I don't want to argue with you," she said, taking a seat in one of the chairs across from his desk."

His brittle smile softened slightly. "Sweetheart, I know

how upsetting this is for you, but the fact is that Jessica's served her time."

"I know that," Natalia snapped. "No matter how many times I hear it—it's not going to change the way I feel. Obviously, we are on opposite sides when it comes to prison reform and Jessica Ricks. I'm going upstairs. I need to respond to some emails."

Upstairs, Natalia thought back to the day of Jessie Belle's funeral. Traynor had been so upset with her because he believed that she'd been responsible for his wife's near-fatal fall. He even had the nerve to confront her during the repast.

"What are you doing here?" he demanded. "I would have thought you'd be smart enough to leave after the burial. I suppose you did all this to gloat."

Natalia ignored the rancor she heard in his voice. "I only came here to pay my respects. I know how much you and Holt loved Jessie Belle."

Traynor gestured for her to follow him to his study. "How dare you show your face here after everything you've done," he uttered, closing the door so they would not be overheard. "Jessie Belle is dead because of you."

Taken aback by his outburst, Natalia uttered, "Excuse me?"

"I know what you did, Natalia, and I want you to know that you are going to pay. If it's the last thing that I do— you're going to pay for this." His voice was stern and filled with anger.

"I don't know what you think I did, but you're wrong about me," she managed to say without stumbling over her

words. Traynor had never talked to her like this. "I didn't do anything to your wife. In case you've forgotten, I once looked at Jessie Belle like a second mother."

"I know about your little visit, Natalia," Traynor interjected. "You know the one where you decided to bring a knife." *He growled the word out between clenched teeth.*

"I only wanted to scare her," *Natalia snapped.* "Traynor, you have no idea what kind of woman you married; my father is dead because of your wife. She blackmailed him to get his church for you. I have proof. The merger was a go as long as Holt and I married and as you know, that didn't happen."

At the time, Traynor did not care what she had to say. He had declared her guilty and that was the end of it. But he had not been the only one who believed that she had harmed Jessie Belle. Mary Ellen had a few things to say to her as well.

Natalia spied Mary Ellen just as she was making her escape.

"What do you want?"

"I'd like to know why you came here today," *Mary Ellen demanded.* "Natalia, this family is going through enough and they certainly don't need you around here causing trouble."

"I simply came to pay my respects and now I'm leaving."

"Stay away from Traynor and Holt."

"They have nothing to fear from me," *she stated.* "As long as they leave me alone."

Mary Ellen met her gaze. "What do you mean by that?"

Folding her arms across her chest, she responded, "Exactly what I said."

"I knew your father; Natalia and he would be so disappointed in the woman you've become. Petty and bitter."

A wave of anger flowed through her at Mary Ellen's comment. "My father is dead because of Jessie Belle. If he were still alive, maybe I would be a different person."

"Jessie Belle is gone, Natalia. "You need to find a way to move on."

By the time she was able to let go of her anger, she found out that her best friend's husband had been found dead in Florida. Charlotte was distraught. Natalia had been stunned to discover that the woman he'd had an affair with was somehow connected to Jessie Belle Deveraux. When Charlotte turned up dead—Natalia was convinced that Jessica, who was going by the name Reina, was the one responsible.

During her quest for answers, Natalia broke into the woman's house searching for proof and stole her diary. It was for that reason, Jessica wanted her dead. She had discovered the truth.

"Jessie Belle Deveraux was your mother."

Jessica's eyes told a story of their own. Although she appeared cordial, her eyes exposed a hidden evil underneath, scaring Natalia. "I don't need an admission from you. I just want you to stop pointing that gun at me and leave my house. If you do that, I'll see that you get your journal back."

A shadow of alarm touched Jessica's face. "You broke into my house? Where is it?"

"I have it someplace safe," Natalia said, *"If you harm me in any way, you will never find it."*

Jessica's gaze conveyed the fury within her. "I want my journal back."

Dear Lord, please don't let me die. Help me... was the last thought Natalia had on that day.

She refused to accept the theory that if she had not broken into Jessica's house and stolen the diary—perhaps none of this would have happened. Natalia refused to accept any responsibility that she went after Jessica first.

It didn't matter, she told herself.

Her motive for breaking into Jessica's house and stealing the diary was to prove that she had murdered Charlotte and Michael.

Chapter 4

AIDEN ST. PAUL greeted his wife with a kiss when she walked out of the bathroom. "Good morning, sweetheart. You look happier than usual."

"I'm very happy," she replied, eying her husband. She still found him incredibly handsome. His complexion, the color of honey, was dotted with a light sprinkle of freckles and complimented his warm brown gaze. "I'm happy that Jessica's home. It's great seeing my sister outside of the prison. She looks great—a little thin, but healthy."

"That's good. I'm sure she's thrilled to have her freedom back. I only hope that she does everything she's supposed to do to stay out of prison."

"I believe she will," Chrissy responded as she sat down on the edge of the bed. "Jessica's changed a lot in the past eight years for the better. She said that she's been called to minister to other women—broken women."

"Really?"

"Yeah," Chrissy answered him thickly. "Why do you look so skeptical?"

"I'm hoping she's right that she was called by God," Aiden said. He pulled a shirt out of the closet and put it on.

"So, you think that God can't use her because of her past?" Chrissy challenged. "Honey, she will be able to reach people that Traynor, Holt or I could never reach—just because of what she's been through... and because of what she's done. Look at me... a former prostitute... God choose me to bring men and women out of that life. Trust me... He can use my sister, too."

"Clayton believes he's been called as well," Aiden said. He selected a tie and slipped it on. "Do you really believe that people are going to follow a former drug dealer and a murderer?"

"He's giving his trial sermon on Sunday. Let's table this conversation for now until after you hear what Clayton has to say."

Aiden agreed. "I have to attend a mixer after work, so don't hold dinner for me."

Chrissy smiled. Not only was he a great husband and father—Aiden was a hard worker. He was recently promoted to Chief Operating Officer of Newton Pharmaceuticals and she was extremely proud of him.

"I'm going to take Caleb and Lenore to meet Jessica today."

He smiled. "They're going to love her. Lenore acts like she already knows her auntie."

Laughing, Chrissy agreed. "Maybe it's because I've

told them so much about her. I feel like the more we surround her with family—the less likely she'll have a relapse."

"Honey, do you think coming back here is the best thing for Jessica?"

"I do," Chrissy responded. "She needs to be around family." She slipped on a pair of jeans and a tank top. "We can hold her accountable for her actions."

"I'm sure Natalia's not pleased with this at all."

"I don't really care how she feels," Chrissy stated, "My sister needs me and I'm going to be there for her."

Chapter 5

"SO, what are you going to do today?" Clayton asked when Jessica came downstairs.

She shrugged in nonchalance. "I don't know. It's not like I have any plans. I think I'll probably work out in the gym, then who knows...."

"I need to meet with Traynor for a couple of hours this morning. After that, you have me all to yourself. I want to go over the businesses with you. Everything is completely legitimate—no money laundering... nothing."

"We'll do that and then afterward, we can grab some sandwiches and go to the park," Jessica suggested. "It's such a beautiful Saturday. We can take our bicycles."

"When do you meet with your probation officer?"

"Monday," she responded.

He set a plate of scrambled eggs, bacon, and toast in front of her.

Jessica settled down in the chair at the breakfast

counter. "I really missed your cooking hon. That prison food—it was edible... that's all I can really say about it."

"I thought about opening a restaurant, but I decided against it—at least in the Raleigh area. If it's a venture you're interested in—we can look into another area."

Jessica shook her head no. "Running a restaurant is a huge commitment. I love cooking, but I don't think it's something I want to do for customers." Clayton was always on the lookout for business opportunities. He firmly believed in having multiple streams of income. He vowed he would never again be poor or living below the poverty level. He took classes to learn about stocks and bonds and Jessica knew that before she went to prison, his portfolio boasted assets worth almost four million dollars. By now, she was sure he had doubled or even tripled that value.

Her own personal net worth was 1.2 million dollars before her arrest. When they sat down together later, Jessica would learn where she was financially.

They made small talk as they ate.

"How did you like sleeping alone in that kind-sized bed?" Clayton inquired, looking her over seductively.

"It was different," Jessica admitted. "I woke up a few times, but then pure exhaustion kind of took over." She took a sip of her orange juice. "You've been sleeping alone for all this time... it might be a bit for you after we get married."

Clayton looked at her. "Is there something you want to ask me?"

"I've been away for eight long years... has there been anyone else?"

"Nothing serious and never in this house," he confessed. "But that was before I turned my life around. I had a tough time dealing with the fact that you were locked up. I wasn't sure we were going to still be together."

"I know. Bae, I don't blame you for anything. I'm grateful you didn't bring it here to my home." Jessica finished off her scrambled eggs.

After Clayton left, she went to their home gym and worked out for the next hour. She found it a healthy way to work out any frustration she might be feeling. She made a mental note to sign up for a kickboxing class.

She had just gotten out of the shower when Clayton returned.

After she got dressed, they went down to his office.

Clayton sat at the desk and Jessica sank down on the black leather loveseat.

"We own a sports team uniform service. We sell uniforms to teams all over the world. The company is based out of Atlanta and it's made us a lot of money."

"Cheerleading uniforms, too?"

He nodded. "We have everything for every sport. I've hired some of the top designers." Clayton pointed to the laptop sitting on the coffee table. "Open the browser. There's a link to JCW Sports."

"Very nice," Jessica murmured.

"We also own Challenger Awards. I figure we can do the awards, uniforms... the whole thing. Besides, when I build my youth center, we can provide these things to the teens for little to no cost."

"You've been talking about that center for years. When are you going to open it?"

"When you see the probation officer, and he asks you about a job, you can tell him that you draw a salary as the CFO for Challenger and JCW Sports. It won't be a lie—the job is yours if you want it. The position is remote—you can work from here."

Jessica looked at him. "Thank you, bae. You are always looking out for me."

"I meant what I said all those years ago. I will always be here for you."

Chapter 6

JESSICA WOKE up a little past nine on Monday morning, to dim light and the sound of rain spattering against her window. It had been years since she had been able to sleep so late. She sat up and swung her feet to the side of the bed.

There was a light knock on the door, then Clayton stuck his head inside. "Hey beautiful... I figured you might want to sleep in this morning. I made chocolate chip pancakes for breakfast."

"Thank you. I'll take a quick shower and join you in a few."

She was meeting her probation officer in a couple of hours. Jessica pushed aside all worries. She was going to trust that God had gone before her and would give her favor with the woman she would be reporting to for the next five years. Jessica had heard several horror stories of ex-cons abused and mistreated by their probation officers.

She slipped on a pair of slacks and a bright-colored

tunic top. They hung loosely on her body because of the weight she had lost.

"After my meeting, I'm going shopping for my wedding gown and I need to find a dress to wear on Sunday for your trial sermon."

"You going alone?"

She shook her head no. "Chrissy's going with me. I'm not up on the latest fashions. I'm also going to pick up some magazines."

Jessica followed him downstairs to the kitchen.

She helped Clayton clean up after they finished eating. Jessica needed to keep busy so that she wouldn't fret over her appointment.

"You okay, babe?"

"Yeah."

"Do you want me to go with you?"

"No, you're supposed to meet with Traynor," Jessica said. "I'll be fine."

An hour and a half later, she felt relieved when she left the judicial building in downtown Raleigh. The meeting had gone well, Jessica decided. Now she was on her way to meet Chrissy at the bridal shop.

Mannequins dressed in white gowns stood in one window, one with a tuxedoed man on her arm. Jessica paused to admire the dress on display before going inside.

Chrissy was already there. "I already saw a couple of gowns I thought you might like."

"Nothing too formal, I hope."

Inside were two solid rooms of formal wear. She followed her sister into the reception area.

"May I help you?" A young woman, dressed in the latest fashion, looked up from the appointment book behind her desk.

"Yes. Chrissy St. Paul, and this is Jessica, the bride. We're shopping for a wedding dress today."

"Congratulations." The woman smiled. Alex was silent as Jennifer, as it stated on her name tag, and Johanna hashed over what sort of style would suit her. Never in her life had she shopped in such a place. All around her were dresses in white and cream satin, some adorned with lace, others with intricate beading and crystals.

Jessica found herself in a changing room, three separate dresses hanging before her. The first two didn't seem quite right, but the third time one possessed a certain charm. She emerged from the changing area smiling. "I like this one."

Standing before the full-length mirror, she fell in love with it. Strapless, the satin bodice was short, gathered in an empire style just beneath her breasts, with a thin strip of satin ribbon marking the seam and the top of the bust line above. Beneath, it flowed gracefully to the floor, a filmy overskirt of organza adding romance to the look. It was simple and stunning.

"I saw a pair of shoes that would be perfect for this dress," Chrissy said, her voice tinged with emotion. "You look beautiful, Jessica," she added, before disappearing out of the room.

When Chrissy returned with the shoes, Jessica tried them on.

"You're right. They're perfect." She eyed her reflection. "I love it."

Jessica bought her gown and shoes. They left the bridal shop and drove to Crabtree Valley Mall.

By lunchtime, their arms were laden with shopping bags. In addition to the footwear and clothes, she'd purchased some new lingerie at the department store.

"I'm famished. Let's have lunch." Chrissy led Jessica over to the restaurant housed on the corner. "I'm so excited about your wedding. I want to have a small reception at my house."

Jessica laughed as a server brought tall glasses of iced water. "It's just going to be us. Don't go through all that trouble and expense. We can just go to a restaurant after the ceremony."

"Are you sure?"

She nodded. "Girl, I'm 43 years old. Clayton and I just want to be married."

Their food arrived.

While they ate, Jessica spotted a woman in the restaurant that reminded her of Gloria Ricks, the person who rescued her from death, but condemned her to a life of hell. Anabeth had taken Jessie Belle to Gloria to get rid of the babies.

Chrissy glanced over her shoulder, then back at Jessica. "What are you staring at?"

"That woman over there looks like Gloria."

"Really?"

Chewing slowly, Jessica nodded. "I will never understand how Anabeth could do that, especially considering she was supposed to be a Christian. She cared more about what people would think of her than the fact that she threw us away like garbage."

"Sis, it's no point in looking back. She's gone so we'll never know what she was thinking and why she did what she did—focus on the future."

"I know you're right, Chrissy. It still bothers me at times when I think about all the physical and verbal abuse I had to endure growing up. She was the root of all our suffering."

"You have to forgive her, Jessica."

She stared down at her plate. "I know you're right and I'm trying. I really am."

"Let's talk about good stuff... like your wedding," Chrissy said, "What type of cake do you want?"

Jessica laughed. "I don't really care—it just needs to have buttercream frosting. Clayton doesn't like cakes with fondant."

Chrissy frowned. "I don't like them either. Do you want any particular filling?"

"No, just pick something."

"This is your wedding cake, Jessica."

She wiped her mouth with her napkin. "Strawberry is fine."

Chrissy broke into a smile. "Thank you."

"I'm not trying to be difficult," Jessica said with a chuckle. "Clayton and I just want to say our vows, then go home and make up for lost time, if you know what I mean. It's been a *long* time."

Chrissy's eyebrows rose in surprise. "You mean you two haven't had sex since you've been home?"

"We decided to wait until our wedding night."

"That's so sweet."

"I wouldn't dare tell him this, but it's been torture," Jessica uttered. "I'm so ready for my wedding night."

"Yeah, let's get you married on Saturday morning. We can celebrate on Sunday."

"Do me a favor and make it as early as possible."

Chapter 7

JESSICA'S WEDDING day dawned clear, with a light blue sky sparsely dotted with fluffy white clouds. The weather was nice--it provided the perfect setting to get married.

Stepping out of the bubbles, she wrapped a thick blue towel around herself and stared in the mirror.

Today she was a bride.

Jessica dried her hair, letting the natural curls spring free as she slipped from the bathroom into her room.

"It's your wedding day," Chrissy announced from the doorway. "Did you get enough sleep?"

Jessica nodded and gave a tiny smile as she sister entered the bedroom.

"Are you okay?" Chrissy touched her shoulder.

The tears came so quickly, so completely unexpectedly, that Jessica was powerless to stop them.

Chrissy came forward, tucking Jessica into her embrace, where she sobbed.

"Sweetie, what's wrong?"

Jessica wiped her face with the back of her hands. "It just really hit me... I'm getting married. Clayton and I have talked about this day for so long... it's really happening."

"Yes, it is."

"I don't think I've ever been so happy."

"You deserve it."

"No, I don't, but I'm so thankful."

"Let's get you dressed," Chrissy said.

There was a soft knock on the door. Frankie stuck her head inside. "I came to help."

Jessica gestured for her sister-in-law to enter. "I can use all the help I can get. The hair stylist isn't here yet and we need to get started. I can do my own hair, but you might have to do my makeup. It's been a while."

Frankie glanced out of the window. "I think your stylist just got here. Is she doing your makeup too?"

"No, her sister was going to do it, but I got a text that she's not feeling well. She texted me from the emergency room."

"Oh wow..."

They were joined by Tiana, who set up quickly to get started on Jessica's hair.

"How's your sister doing?" Chrissy inquired.

"She has some type of stomach bug. They are giving her fluids right now. I'm going to the hospital as soon as I'm done with Jessica's hair. I need to get my nephew."

When Tiana was done, Frankie performed her magic with foundation, powder, eye shadow and blush. She applied a matte lipstick in a soft chai color as the finishing touch.

Traynor's wife, Angela joined them as Tiana packed up to leave.

"Thank you," Jessica said, handing a hundred-dollar bill to the stylist. "Give your sister a hug from me. I hope she feels better soon."

"I will. Enjoy your special day."

Jessica looked in the mirror at her reflection and wanted to cry a second time. Her ice green eyes were large, and more luminous than she could have imagined, while her smooth complexion appeared flawless. Her warm brown hair was pulled back gently from the sides, the rest curling down her back. A small circlet of flowers sat daintily on her head.

"I look like a bride." She touched a finger to her cheek.

"A very beautiful bride," Chrissy responded. "All you need now is something borrowed and something blue. Then you'll be all set to walk down the aisle."

Jessica broke into a grin. "I am not some young, blushing bride. I don't need all that stuff."

"Your sister's right." Angela, dressed in a pale lavender suit, opened her clutch handbag, and took out a small box. "This should cover the *borrowed* and *blue* part."

Jessica opened the lid and found a square velvet box. Inside was a sapphire and diamond necklace and earring set. Tiny diamonds surrounded the oval stones. "They're gorgeous."

"My first husband gave them to me on our tenth anniversary. I'd hoped my daughter would one day wear them on her wedding day... she's gone now... I'd like for you to wear them."

"Are you sure?" Jessica asked.

"I'd be honored if you'd wear them."

Jessica carefully removed the earrings. She held up the necklace and Angela fastened it around her neck.

"Ready?" Chrissy asked.

Jessica nodded.

In the backyard, the portable arch was in place, and the white folding chairs, numbering twenty, were in small, precise rows. Leaned up against the deck were four long, foldable tables that tomorrow would be adorned with white tablecloths, all borrowed from the church.

Frankie played a song on her iPhone for Jessica to walk down the grassy aisle.

Clayton turned when the music started, and she paused as their eyes met. His brows lifted briefly in surprise, then a huge smile of approval swept over his face, the heat of it tangible even from several feet away.

She stopped when he took three steps out of position and lifted his hand, offering it to her.

She took it.

"You look beautiful," he whispered, making her heart swell. He led her under the arch and before Traynor, to begin their life together.

Chapter 8

"YOU LOOK BEAUTIFUL MRS. WALLACE."

Jessica laughed. "Thank you, husband. Are you nervous about today?"

"No, not really," Clayton responded. "I'm going to do what Traynor told me—just speak from my heart."

"I have faith in you."

They left for the church ten minutes later.

Angela was waiting for them outside. After a quick embrace, she told Clayton, "Traynor's wants you to come to the office. He wants to pray with you."

When he left, she smiled at Jessica. "I hope you two managed to get some rest."

"Not much. I think Clayton's running on adrenaline. He's very excited about this day. I remember a time when he wouldn't be caught inside of a church. He didn't even want to have a funeral service in one."

"Look at God," Angela said.

"Is Holt and my sister here?" Deep down, Jessica was

anxious about stepping back into Bright Hope. Michael Jennings was the pastor before Traynor took over. She was sure some of the church members would remember her and more importantly—her crimes. Jessica prayed that those who remembered her would not judge Clayton for her wrongdoing.

"Yes, they're in the office with Traynor. All the ministers and associate pastors are in there to pray over Clayton. Aiden and the kids should be arriving any moment."

"So, Frankie's already inside?"

Angela nodded. "Yes, we're going to sit with them."

Jessica hesitated.

"What is it, dear?"

"I don't want to ruin this for Clayton. Eight years isn't long enough for members of this church to have forgotten what I've done."

"You hold your head up high, Jessica. Your husband is going to need you sitting near the front. He needs your support. Don't you worry about anything else."

"I'm ready."

They entered the sanctuary of Bright Hope and took their seats.

Jessica could feel the heat of the stares stabbing at her but continued to look straight ahead, but her stomach quivered with apprehension. When she had called Traynor to discuss her concerns about coming, he had reassured her that she would be welcomed with open arms. She knew that Bright Hope had a successful prison ministry and often, former inmates would visit the church upon release. A few had even become members.

Jessica forced her thoughts from her to Clayton. She knew how much time he had put in on his sermon. She sent up a quick prayer that his words would reach those who needed it the most.

Including me, she thought.

The moment arrived for Clayton to speak.

He walked up to the podium in confidence, his smile brilliant and sincere. "Good morning," he greeted.

The congregation responded in kind.

"I'm sure some of you are wondering who I am. Sure, you've seen me here on Sunday and most times at Bible Study, but what do you really know about me? I will say this—I do not look like what I've been through. I am not the same man I was five years ago. When I was growing up, we never went to church. We never had a Bible. My family never talked about God except to blame Him for everything bad that happened. The first time I heard about Christianity, I was eight years old. I had a friend who invited me to Vacation Bible School. I had to beg my mama to let me go." He paused a moment, then said, "I became fascinated by the concept of God—not enough for me to want to attend church or pick up a Bible, but I remember looking forward to going to VBS every summer until I was 13 years old. After that, my summers were spent partying, selling drugs and everything else you do when you don't have God in your life."

Jessica met his gaze and smiled, silently urging him to continue. Her eyes then traveled the room. Clayton had everyone's attention. They looked engaged and eager to hear what he had to say.

"I walked around with gangs, and I started robbing other drug dealers in the area... I had so much money I didn't know what to do with it, I had a good woman, but I wasn't happy. I felt as if there was something missing. Five years ago, I came here to see Pastor Deveraux. As soon as I walked into his office, I got down on my knees and cried like a baby. My wife don't even know this, but I was at the point of suicide and I needed a sign to continue living."

Jessica released a soft gasp.

Frankie reached over and gave her hand a gentle squeeze.

"Pastor Deveraux challenged me to examine my doubts, read the Bible, pray, and think about the implications of what I believed about life and God. I began to wrestle with the existence of God, scientifically and philosophically, and questions of suffering and evil that came from my own experience. I wrestled with the reliability of the Bible, the legitimacy of miracles, and the dark history of the church—which I felt was filled with judgment, violence, and hypocrisy. The more I explored, the more I saw the emotional power and soundness of Christianity."

Angela leaned over and whispered, "He's doing a fantastic job."

"It was in Vacation Bible School that I first heard the call of God to preach the Gospel. I didn't take it seriously because I considered myself a failure. I convinced myself that God couldn't use someone like me. But five years ago, I learned that God can and will use broken men and women to fulfill His perfect plan."

"Amen," Jessica murmured.

"One of the first stories, Pastor Deveraux had me read was the story of the prodigal son. This story shows that God gives His best even to failures. This is the message of the Gospel—redemption and a new beginning. Not just once, but repeatedly. God never gives up on anyone. The parable in Matthew 20 teaches us the same thing. People hired last were the ones rewarded first. In other words, those who had wasted 90% of their lives, doing nothing of eternal value, could still do something glorious for God with the remaining 10% of their lives. This should be tremendous encouragement to all of us."

At the end of Clayton's sermon, he received a standing ovation.

Jessica had taken a lot of nuggets from his message. She really liked the visual of a ball of string so knotted that one has no hope of untying the knots and how Jesus has come to untie every one of those knots.

Chrissy walked over to her smiling. "Clayton did such a wonderful job, sis."

She agreed. "I'm so proud of him."

"I loved the message that we can all learn from our failures and go on to fulfill God's perfect plan for our lives. Then bro-in-law drove the point home when he said he was living proof that no one is beyond the reach of God. *Amen.*"

Jessica smiled. "I couldn't stop my tears when he was officially ordained as a minister."

"He's worked five years for this," Chrissy told her.

"I'm really happy for him. I don't know if he's told you, but he just got accepted to Duke Divinity School."

Clayton had surprised her on their wedding night when he showed her his degree in Psychology. He then told her about the acceptance letter.

"That's great news."

"Things are really taking off for Clayton," Jessica said.

"The same is going to happen for you, sis."

They were joined by Caleb and Lenore who were ready to leave.

"Can we go get ice cream?" Lenore asked.

"Maybe later," Chrissy responded. "We're going to Auntie Jessica's house for dinner."

Jessica wrapped an arm around her niece. "I have some ice cream in the fridge. After we eat, I'm sure your mom and dad won't mind if you have some."

"Do you have mint chocolate chip?" Caleb inquired.

"I sure do," she responded. "We have strawberry, vanilla and I think one more."

Lenore jumped up and down excitedly. "We're gonna have ice cream... gonna have ice cream..."

Chapter 9

JESSICA EYED her reflection in the full-length mirror. They were getting ready for bed and she was wearing a piece of lingerie, she'd purchased right before their wedding.

"You look beautiful," Clayton said from behind her. "You could've been a model."

She had heard that sentiment many times over the years, but Jessica had no interest in gracing runways or magazines. She finished off her Champagne, then walked over to Clayton who was standing by the fireplace. Jessica watched his broad shoulders heaving as he breathed, the vision sending shivers of delight through her.

He swung her into the circle of his arms and kissed her. "I'm so glad this day is ending. With the sermon out of the way, I can now focus on you."

Jessica gave him a sensuous look. "Do you really want to spend all this time talking?" she asked playfully.

Grinning, Clayton shook his head. Without another word, he picked her up and carried her over to their bed.

Chapter 10

"HELLO DAUGHTER."

"Jessie Belle..." Jessica glanced around. She looked to be in a park somewhere. "Where are we?"

"Wherever you want to be."

"I never figured on talking to you again."

"But you want to talk to me."

"I wanted a lot of things," Jessica murmured. "None of it matters anymore."

"You're finally at peace."

"In some areas," she said. "In others... I'm still working on it. I have a husband who loves me—Clayton has loved me most of my life. I finally have the family that I've always wanted, but I caused so much pain to get it."

"I caused a lot of pain during my lifetime—I know that feeling. God forgave me. He gave me a second chance just like He's given you. Don't waste it looking back in the rearview mirror."

"I don't think I've ever asked you to forgive me, Jessie Belle."

"There is nothing to forgive. I'm the one who needs your forgiveness. I should've fought for my children."

"Like you said, it does no good to keep reliving the past. I just wanted you to know that I know my purpose now. I was called to minister to women like me—broken women."

Jessica opened her eyes; her gaze was met with darkness. She felt a wave of disappointment wash over her. It was nothing more than a dream. She glanced over at Clayton who was sound asleep, his chest rising and falling to the rhythm of his breathing.

"Jessie Belle, why do I keep dreaming about you?" she whispered. "I wanted you to be a part of my life when you were among the living. I don't need you now."

Chapter 11

"CHRISSY, MY DAUGHTER..."

"Jessie Belle?" She glanced around. They were back in the old house—the one where Chrissy had pushed her mother over the balcony.

"You're remembering that night."

Chrissy nodded. "I was wrong for doing that to you. I was in a bad space back then."

Jessie Belle reached over and covered her hand with her own. "I understand, my precious child. I'd done some terrible things to you and I pray that you can forgive me."

"I forgave you a long time ago. That's partly why I don't understand what's going on now. Why are we here?"

"Have you not yearned to talk to me?"

Chrissy smiled. "I have. I wanted to tell you about my wonderful husband and my children. I have a son named Caleb and my daughter's name is Lenore."

"I wish I could see them—all of my grandbabies. I've

missed so much of my own children's lives... it doesn't seem fair, but... her voice died.

"I always think of you looking down from heaven. It gives me a certain sense of peace to think of you in that way."

"I'm glad that you allow me into your thoughts."

"We all miss you, Jessie Belle."

Her mother looked as if she were about to get emotional. "I'm sorry... what you said—it's more than I deserve."

"None of us are perfect. Well... except Traynor and Holt. We've all messed up badly. The beauty is that God loves us despite our flaws."

"Tell me more about the children..."

Chapter 12

CHRISSY STRODE into Brown and Barton Real Estate with her morning cup of coffee and two more for her partner and office manager. She was usually the first to arrive on Monday mornings. She preferred to plan out the rest of her week in solitude.

Humming softly, she sat down at her desk and turned on her computer. While waiting for it to boot up, Chrissy checked her voice messages.

She smoothed her auburn hair with her hand as her eyes traveled her office. Chrissy was thankful for all God had blessed her with—her business, her family, and her ministry. The journey from prostitution to dealing with being bipolar to becoming a Christian was her testimony, and her ministry.

She opened her planner but found it hard to focus, her mind was suddenly consumed with the dream she'd had of Jessie Belle the night before. *It seemed so real. Like I was really with her.*

"Good morning," Sabrina greeted, cutting into her thoughts.

"Hey you," Chrissy responded. "I have your mocha latte."

"Thank you so much. I need it. I don't know why but I'm tired."

"Late night?"

Sabrina broke into a grin. "It wasn't that late. Eric and I watched a movie and then we just talked—before I realized it, it was almost one a.m."

Chrissy raised an eyebrow. "You're really liking this guy."

She nodded. "I do, but I haven't told him about my old life."

"How long have you two been dating?"

"Six months," Sabrina responded. "He says that he's ready to settle down and he feels that

I'm the woman for him."

"Then you need to be honest with him."

"I intend to—I just don't know when." Sabrina sat down at her desk. "I have to say that I'm afraid I'm going to lose him though. I don't know if he can handle knowing that I was once a prostitute."

"I once felt the same way about Aiden."

"It worked out for you, Chrissy. I'm just not as confident that it will be the same for me and Eric."

"Then you may have to consider that he isn't the man for you."

Sabrina nodded in agreement. "You're right."

Patty Brown strode through the doors of the real estate

office in a huff. "Can you believe that I got a speeding ticket? I wasn't even going that fast."

Chrissy bit back her smile. "That's the second one in a month."

"This is the last thing I need." She walked over to Chrissy's desk. "I hope that coffee is for me. I need it."

"It's yours."

Patty grabbed it and stalked into her office, closing the door behind her.

"I don't know why she gets so upset," Sabrina said when she entered Chrissy's office. "She knows she was speeding."

Chrissy chuckled.

Shortly before noon, the doors to the office opened.

"Jessica, hi..." Chrissy heard Sabrina say.

She pushed away from her desk and walked out into the reception area. "This is a pleasant surprise." Her eyes strayed to Sabrina, trying to gauge her reaction.

"Welcome home."

Jessica smiled. "Thank you for saying that, Sabrina."

"I mean it. I'm glad you're home."

"What's up?" Chrissy asked.

"I was in the area, so I thought I'd take you to lunch if you have some time."

"Let me grab my purse."

They walked to a nearby restaurant.

When they were seated, Jessica said, "I had a dream last night. I saw her... Jessie Belle."

Chrissy looked surprised. "Are you serious?"

"Yeah... why?"

"I had a dream about her as well. Tell me about yours first."

"We were in a beautiful garden. She said she came because I wanted to talk to her. I told her that I'd finally found my purpose." Jessica eyed Chrissy. "What was your dream about?"

"We were in the house... the one ..."

"I know," Jessica said gently.

"She came to me for the same reason. To talk. In my dream, she asked me to forgive her. It was like she was trying to let me know that she forgave me. I told her about Aiden and the children.

I felt like we talked for hours."

"It was the same for me." Jessica took a sip of her water. "It didn't feel like a dream."

Chrissy nodded in agreement. "What do you think it means?"

"That we both wanted a relationship with our mother. Now that she's gone, we are able to have that in our dreams."

"Do you think we're crazy?"

"Girl, no..."

"Well look at this," a voice from behind her said. "I knew we'd run into each other at some point."

Jessica knew exactly to whom the voice belonged. "Hello Natalia," she said, without turning around.

"How did you know we were here?" Chrissy asked, glaring at Sabrina who responded, "I had no idea where you had gone to eat. Natalia and I made this lunch date last week."

"I hear you're trying to follow in Traynor and your sister's footsteps," Natalia stated loud enough to garner the attention of everyone around them. "You're no minister, Jessica. You're nothing more than a *murderer*."

Sabrina looked embarrassed. "I'm sorry. I didn't know you were coming here." She glanced at her cousin. "We should leave."

"You don't have to go." Chrissy grabbed her purse. "We'll leave."

"I can't believe y'all are buying into this act."

"Natalia, I know that you're upset, but I'm not gonna stand here and let you just attack my sister," Chrissy uttered. "She's accepted responsibility for her actions and she's done her time. Now leave her alone."

"Wow..." Natalia uttered while eyeing Jessica. "You've really got her fooled. I just hope she doesn't end up paying with her life."

Jessica felt the urge to choke Natalia but resisted. She kept reminding herself that the woman had every right to be angry with her.

"What? You don't have anything to say?"

This chick is taunting me. Lord, I know I was wrong, but I need you to please get me away from Natalia. I can only take so much of her mouth. Jessica turned and walked toward the exit door, praying that Natalia would have the good sense not to follow her.

"I'm proud of you," Chrissy said when they were outside.

"Don't be," Jessica responded. "I wanted to smack her."

"How would you like to spend some time with your

niece and nephew?" Chrissy inquired. "Dean and I have a date tonight and I was going to call my babysitter, but if you're interested—"

"Really? I'd love it," she responded. Jessica was already in love with Caleb and Lenore. She adored all her nieces and nephews. They were the closest she would ever get to having children of her own, so she intended to spoil them like any other favorite aunt. "Now Clayton will have to brush up on his video game skills. He bought an X-Box and a bunch of games for whenever the kids come over."

Chrissy chuckled. "Caleb and Holt Jr. both adore their uncle."

"Trust me... he feels the same way about them."

Jessica's thoughts turned to Natalia and the way she'd just humiliated her in that restaurant.

She clenched and unclenched her fists. A spark of anger ignited into full-fledged fury. By the time Chrissy dropped her back to her car, Jessica was ready to go back and confront Natalia.

"So, I'll drop the kids off at six," Chrissy said, cutting into her thoughts. "Is that okay?"

She nodded. "It's perfect. I'll see you then."

"Jessica... go straight home."

"I am."

"She's not worth it. You've come too far."

"Thanks Chrissy." She was grateful for her sister's attempt to talk her off the ledge of what could very well send her back to prison. *Chrissy's right. She's not worth my freedom.*

Chapter 13

NATALIA GLANCED over at her cousin. "What?" She couldn't understand why Sabrina was looking at her as if she'd done something wrong. She wasn't the one who had committed several major felonies.

"I can't believe you just did that," Sabrina said after they settled in a booth. "You know there was a time when you were selfish and even a bit cruel—you did some terrible things to people, but people were willing to give you a second chance." Her tone was coolly disapproving.

Tossing her hair across her shoulders in a gesture of defiance, Natalia responded, "I never murdered anyone."

"You can kill someone with your words. What right do you have to attack Jessica the way you just did?"

A waiter walked over with their orders before Natalia could respond.

"Did you forget what she did to me?" she asked, each word displaying her anger. She could barely hold her tongue while waiting for the server to leave.

"No, I remember. We will all remember because you're never going to let anyone forget it."

Shaking her head, Natalia uttered, "I can't believe this..."

"At some point, you're gonna have to forgive her. What she did to you—it was wrong, but God protected you. The same God who loves you also loves her. The old Reina... I mean Jessica... she would've given as good as she got, but she didn't say a word."

"That's only because she's on probation and Jessica knows I'll do whatever to have her hauled back off to prison. She's no longer the one in control." Natalia made a mental note to find out the name of Jessica's probation officer.

Sabrina interrupted her thoughts. "And you are not her judge."

Natalia stiffened in her seat. "I know you are a wannabe Bible scholar, but you need to make sure you know what it says."

"We often mistake what the Bible actually says about judging others. The Bible states that there are two ways to judge others," Sabrina responded. "One way is to judge the motives of others—this is sinful. The other way is judging their actions, which is the right thing to do. You've read the book of Matthew... what is Jesus talking about during his Sermon on the Mount?"

"He talks about motives."

"In Matthew 7:1-2, Jesus clearly states we are not to judge other people's motives. We know Jesus must be talking about motives in that scripture because Scripture never contradicts Scripture. He is telling us that once we address our own sin—we are then to *help* people with their sin. Throughout the Sermon on the Mount, Jesus was explaining that it was impossible for people to save themselves—even if they obeyed the law perfectly, their hearts and motivations were still sinful. Natalia, if our salvation was based upon the inner righteousness we have on our own—girl, we'd be doomed. You know I'm right."

"It's her actions that I am judging," she insisted archly.

Matthew 7, verses 3-5 says, "*Why do you see the speck that is in your brother's eye, but do not notice the log that is in your own eye? Or how can you say to your brother, 'Let me take the speck out of your eye,' when there is the log in your own eye? You hypocrite, first take the log out of your own eye, and then you will see clearly to take the speck out of your brother's eye.*"

"I know that the Bibles tells us to be careful when we are judging the actions of others, Sabrina. I know that we should spend our time going over our own actions."

"Then you should agree that it's wrong to judge others when we have sin in our own lives. Even Paul talks about this in 1 Corinthians 4, verses 4 and 5. "*It is the Lord who judges me. Therefore, do not pronounce judgment before the time, before the Lord comes, who will bring to light the things now hidden in darkness and will disclose the purposes of the heart.*"

Natalia sighed. "I hear what you're saying, but I don't agree."

"You need to leave Jessica to God. He is the ultimate judge."

"And you need to remember that blood is thicker than water. Why don't you come work with me at the law office? I can use a good office manager."

"I happen to enjoy working at Brown and Barton. I don't see any reason for having to leave a job I love."

"I'll match whatever you're making over there."

"It's not about the money, Natalia. I love my job. I can't believe that you're being so petty right now."

Chapter 14

JESSICA SLAMMED the front door behind her. She breathed in shallow, quick gasps.

Clayton met her in the living room. "What's wrong?"

She was surprised to find him at home. "I thought you'd still be with Traynor." Jessica couldn't control the spasmodic trembling within her. She was furious. She wanted to go after Natalia—to make her pay for humiliating her in that restaurant. She could feel the edges of her self-control becoming unraveled.

"Babe, what happened? Talk to me."

It took Jessica a few minutes to calm herself.

"After I checked in with my probation officer, I stopped by Chrissy's office and invited her to lunch. We ran into Natalia."

Clayton gestured for her to sit down on the sofa.

He sat down beside her and began rubbing her back, soothing Jessica.

"In the middle of the restaurant, she called me a

murderer. I couldn't do anything but take it, Clayton." Tears escaped from her eyes and rolled down her cheeks. "I've worked so hard to change. All I want to do now is help others, but Natalia's going to do everything in her power to ruin that for me. I'm not going to be able to do anything as long as I stay here in Raleigh."

His eyes widened in surprise. "You want to move?"

Jessica shook her head. "Not really. I love spending time with my family, but I'm not going to have any peace in this town." She wiped her face with the back of her hand. "She was talking loud so everyone could hear—I wanted to snatch her tongue out."

"You are not that person any more. One day Natalia will see this for herself." Clayton pulled her into his arms. "As for you, wife... you have to continue seeing yourself as God sees you. Stay focused and determined, babe. You've already made it through the darkest part, keep heading toward the light at the end of the tunnel."

She looked at him. "I'm trying, Clayton. Before I was released, the Chaplain told me that I should expect to face change and adversity. He told me that in the eyes of many, I would never be nothing more than a criminal. Society is quick to take the ex-felon label and run with it."

"That's why you have to show that you are just as capable and worthy of being productive members of society as anyone. It's up to you to change the stigma that comes with being labeled an ex-felon."

She struggled to hold her raw emotion in check. "I have to live with my past—I don't need Natalia showing up everywhere I go, shouting murderer." The tight knot within her begged for release.

"I can have a talk with her husband. Maybe he can get her to leave you alone."

"I love you, Clayton. But you don't have to do that."

"I love you, too." His expression darkened with an unreadable emotion. "I won't say anything for now, but if she continues—I'ma need Dean to control his wife."

Jessica settled back, enjoying the feel of his arms around her.

Her eyelids grew heavy and she gave way to sleep.

She awoke with a start at the sound of Clayton's cell phone ringing. Jessica glanced at the clock, and estimated that she'd been sleeping for almost an hour.

"Hey Nikko... what's up?" Clayton greeted groggily.

He had been sleeping as well. She felt his body shift and sat up. Jessica watched as his expression changed to anger.

"When did it happen? Do you know who's responsible?"

She knew Clayton was no longer in that life, but something terrible must have happened. As far as she knew, he and Nikko hadn't talked much since Clayton turned over his operation to him.

When he hung up, he looked at her. "Miquel is dead," he said in a low, tormented voice. "He was shot outside a club. Earlier tonight, Nikko received a phone call telling him to warn me to watch my back."

"But you left that life behind years ago. Who could

possibly want to harm you?" Jessica met his gaze. "You are out, *right*?"

"Yes," Clayton responded. "I haven't looked back once, but I had enemies... apparently, I still have a few."

She felt a dull ache of foreboding. "Are we in danger?"

He shook his head. "Sweetheart, we're fine. There's nothing to worry about."

"Nikko has no idea who killed Miguel?"

"He doesn't," Clayton stated, "He needs to be careful as well. Whoever shot Miguel could be after him."

"I know you want to go to New York to say goodbye to your friend, but I don't think it's a good idea."

He did not comment.

"Clayton, it's a bad idea."

His eyes darkened with pain and grief. "Nikko said the same thing."

"Please tell me that you're not going."

Her words were met with silence.

Chapter 15

THE RICH INTERIOR of mahogany wood, brass fixtures, and Tiffany-style lamps of McCormick & Schmick's Seafood & Steaks nestled in the heart of Crabtree Valley Mall, created an inviting, upscale, yet unpretentious atmosphere. It was a favorite for Chrissy and Aiden on date night.

"I love you," Chrissy said after their waiter left with their food orders. "I really appreciate your trusting me about giving my sister a second chance. When you met me, you got a lot more than you were bargaining for."

"No family is perfect, sweetheart," Aiden said. "I have a cousin who went to prison for killing a man. He was 21 years old and we were like brothers. He was a couple of years older than me. Chucky served 10 years and when he came out, he was a different person. It wasn't easy for him because of the ex-con label, but Chucky didn't let that stop him. He learned how to bake in prison and he turned that skill into a business."

"You've mentioned a few times over the years. Are you two still close?"

"He passed away two years later. He had cancer."

"I'm so sorry."

"He gave his life to the Lord, so I know I'll see him again one day." Aiden broke into a smile. "That boy there could make a lemon pound cake that would make you cry."

"Well, you know baking is not my thing as much as I love sweets."

"I didn't marry you for your skills in the kitchen."

Chrissy grinned. "You have a gift of always knowing the right things to say."

Their food arrived.

Aiden said a blessing over their food.

"Amen," she murmured before sampling the seared sea scallops. "This is delicious."

"So is the blackened chicken fettuccini."

"I love our date nights." Chrissy stuck a forkful of crab potato hash into her mouth. She closed her eyes as she savored her meal.

Aiden wiped his mouth with the edge of his napkin. "I wonder how Clayton and Jessica are faring with the kids."

"I'm sure they're fine. They might be a little tired afterward."

He gave a short laugh. "Lenore's nothing but a ball of energy. That's my baby though."

Chrissy took a sip of water before saying, "You know at my age, I thought I was going through peri-menopause with the headaches, fatigue and mood swings, so I made an appointment to see my doctor. She had a last-minute cancellation, so I left the office at three to see her."

Aiden twirled fettuccini drenched in a Cajun cream sauce around his fork. "So, what did she say?"

"I'm definitely not menopausal."

"Did she tell you that you need to slow down at work? The new office will be open soon. You and Pattie need to hire more agents."

"We're interviewing next week," Chrissy announced. "Sabrina just hired a full-time receptionist. I'm going to cut back on my hours—I'm thinking that I should go into the office three days a week for a while."

Aiden looked at her. "What brought this on? After the kids started school, I figured you working part-time was over."

"Things change," she murmured. "Honey, I'm going to have a baby."

Aiden almost choked on his tea. "Come again?"

Chrissy burst into laughter at the expression on his face. "You okay?"

"We're *pregnant*?"

"Yes, if you want to put it that way. I had given up hope a long time ago that I'd ever conceive a child." Her eyes filled with tears. Blinking rapidly, she said, "I said I wasn't going to get all emotional."

Smiling, Aiden reached over and took her hand in his. "God is good... like he did Abraham and Sarah—he's blessed us with a child."

"So, you're happy about this?"

"Of course. I'm ecstatic, sweetheart." He gave a short laugh. "We're having a baby."

"For now, I'd like to keep it just between us. The pregnancy is high-risk... and it's recommended that we go through genetic testing. However, my doctor says that the actual percentage for down syndrome is less than 3%."

"Honey, we are going to do whatever we have to do to make sure you deliver a healthy baby, but our faith is in the Lord—not the doctor." His eyes grew wet with unshed tears. "We are going to love this gift from God no matter what."

"Amen," Chrissy murmured in response. "I'm forty-three years old and pregnant. Lord have mercy." She glanced around. "I feel like I need a drink right now."

They burst into laughter.

When they left the restaurant forty-five minutes later, Aiden asked, "Are you sure you want to wait on telling the rest of the family? I feel like this is the kind of news we can all use right now. We can hold off on telling the children though."

"I think you're right," Chrissy said. "Let's tell Jessica and Clayton when we get to the house. This will be a fantastic way to end the day, especially after running into Natalia earlier." Shaking her head, she added, "She's gunning for my sister."

"You need to let Jessica deal with this," Aiden said, "I don't want you getting all stressed out."

Chapter 16

"DID YOU HAVE ANY PROBLEMS?" Chrissy asked when they arrived at Jessica's house.

"None at all," she responded. "We had a great time with them. They're in the kitchen now baking cookies with Clayton."

"He bakes, too? I know the man can cook."

Jessica nodded. "We both love cooking."

"There's something I have to tell you," Chrissy said. "I saw my doctor earlier."

"Are you okay?"

"I'm going to have a baby."

Jessica's mouth dropped open in her shock. "You... you're pregnant?"

"I am. It's as much a surprise to me as it is to you, but Aiden and I are over the moon."

She embraced her sister, then Aiden. "I'm so happy for you both. Thank you for sharing this with me."

"You're the first person we've told."

"Do you mind if I tell Clayton?"

"No, we don't mind at all. We're planning to tell Traynor, Holt and everyone else tomorrow. The only thing is that we want to wait until after the first trimester to tell Caleb and Lenore. They've been wanting a sibling for a while now."

"I won't say a word," Jessica promised. "This is wonderful news—much needed after the day we've had. Do you remember Miguel?"

"Yes," Chrissy and Aiden said in unison.

"He was shot last night. He died earlier today."

"Oh no," Chrissy uttered. "I'm so sorry to hear this."

"He's planning to attend the funeral. I don't think it's a good idea, but Clayton has always been a loyal friend. He's promised me that he plans to get on the next flight home right after the service."

"All you can do is just pray for him," Chrissy responded. "We don't turn our back on the people we care about even though we've given our life to Christ."

"I know. I just feel in my spirit that he shouldn't go. I'm not worried that he's going to go back to that life—but once Clayton makes up his mind about something—it's the gospel."

"Did I hear my name?"

Jessica glanced over her shoulder. "Yes, you did, sweetheart. I'm talking about you, love of my life."

He kissed her cheek. "I'll be home before you have a chance to miss me."

They were interrupted by laughter as Caleb and Lenore rushed into the foyer.

"We made oatmeal cookies," Lenore announced. "Uncle Clay packed some up for you and Daddy."

When Chrissy and her family left for home, Jessica went upstairs to take a bath.

She walked out of the bathroom, draped in a fluffy towel to find Clayton sitting on the edge of the bed.

"Babe, you have nothing to worry about. I just want to say goodbye to my friend."

"Clayton, you've been pretty lucky. You were arrested once for transporting drugs. You went away for four years. You were twenty-five at the time. After that, you managed to be in that life and not get caught. You and I both know that there are going to be so many undercover agents taking pictures of everyone attending that funeral. Miguel and Nikko did a lot of the work for you—the feds know about them. Do you really want to have them sniffing around you? Because if you go—that's exactly what is going to happen."

"I won't go to the funeral then," he said. "I'll just go to the funeral home to say my farewell. Then I'll hop on a plane and come straight home."

"There's no changing your mind, is there?"

"Babe, he was my friend."

"And I'm your wife."

Chapter 17

"I ASKED Sabrina to come work with us and she turned me down," Natalia announced that evening as they prepared for bed.

Dean looked up at her. "She seems to like where she works. I'm sure we'll find an office manager soon."

"That's not the point."

"Okay, so what *is* the point?" he asked, propping his back against his king-sized pillow.

"She works with Chrissy."

"And..."

"And Jessica is her sister," Natalia explained. "It's like she's working for the enemy."

Dean's irritation with her was evident. "She's worked there for years. Why do you suddenly have a problem with it?"

Natalia glared at him. "Why do you have to be so difficult?"

"Why do we have to keep talking about Jessica?" he snapped in anger.

"Because she tried to kill me—is that a good enough reason? Or don't you care about that?"

A flash of anger colored his gaze but disappeared as quickly as it had come. "I'm not doing this with you."

He climbed out of bed, slipped on his slippers, and headed toward the door.

"Where are you going?" Natalia demanded.

"Downstairs. I'm going to watch some television."

He was angry with her. In all the years they had been married, Dean had never been so upset with her. This is Jessica's fault, she decided.

"I can't let you destroy my marriage," she whispered to the empty room.

Natalia eased out of bed and went after Dean. She was not going to end the day with this distance between them.

He was in the family room watching some documentary on NBA players.

She sank down beside him. "I'm sorry, Dean."

He placed an arm around her. "I miss this."

"So, do I," Natalia said. "Right now, all I want is for you to come to bed." She gave him a seductive smile. "We don't have to talk."

Dean broke into a grin. "You think all you have to do is bat those pretty eyes and I'm going to do your bidding, don't you?"

"Is it working?"

"Let's go to bed..."

Chapter 18

"LOOK OUT! It's coming in too fast!"

She turned back to see airline employees and travelers gaping at the sky. A plane was silently torpedoing toward the runway. She screamed as it shattered into the runway, the impact vibrating through her bones. Before she could get her feet to move, the plane exploded, flames bustling around it like a parachute that had finally caught wind. "Clay—!"

Jessica shot up in bed, her body trembling.

It was just a dream... a nightmare.

Clayton had taken a late flight the night before. He'd called her as soon as the plane landed, so she knew deep down that he was in his hotel room and probably sound asleep. Jessica knew that he would be returning home later today, but she couldn't shake the nervous energy in her belly. She glanced over at the clock.

Three-thirty a.m.

Jessica opened the drawer of her nightstand and

retrieved a bottle of pills. She opened it and popped one into her mouth, washing it down with water. She turned on the television, hoping to find something to take her mind off Clayton.

She considered calling him just to hear his voice but resisted the urge. He needed to be well-rested for the funeral.

"Father God, please protect my husband," she prayed. "Please let him come back home safe."

I need to pull it together, she chided herself. *The Lord's not done with Clayton yet. He hasn't fulfilled his purpose, so he's going to be fine. I have faith that God will protect him.*

Jessica did not fall asleep until sometime past five o'clock. When she couldn't find anything on TV to watch, she cut it off and read several passages of scripture.

When she woke up, it was eight-fifteen. Jessica checked her phone to see if Clayton had called. He hadn't, but had sent her a text instead saying:

Good morning, babe. Don't worry, I'll be fine. My flight gets in at noon. See you then. Love you.

She sent him a quick response before getting out of bed and navigating to the bathroom.

Inside the shower, the blast of rippling hot water forced her completely awake.

Jessica had just walked out of the bathroom when she heard the front door open and close.

She froze. It was 8:45.

He had gotten rid of the guns. As part of her probation, there could not be any weapons in the house. Panic shot through Jessica. She was about to call 9-1-1 when she heard, "Honey, where are you?"

"In the bedroom," she responded as she walked into the hall. "Clayton, what happened? Your text said that you wouldn't be arriving until later."

"I got ready to meet Nikko and head over to the funeral home, but then the Holy Spirit told me to head straight to the airport. I grabbed my bag and left."

Jessica embraced him. "I know how much you wanted to say goodbye to Miguel, but I have to say that I'm so glad you're home. I didn't have a good feeling about it—you've left that life behind and you need to leave it there."

"I called Nikko and told him that I wouldn't be able to attend, and he understood."

"You did the right thing."

"I know." His voice broke as he grabbed his luggage. "I just wish Miguel was still here. He was like a brother to me."

Jessica slipped her hand into his and felt his trembling. "Why don't you get comfortable. I'll make us a nice lunch and we can just relax for the rest of the day."

"Sounds good to me."

"I love you."

He smiled. "I love you, too."

"Miguel knew how you felt about him. That's just his body in that coffin. He's not there."

"You're right. It still hurts though—maybe if it had been natural causes or something..."

Jessica thought about Michael, Charlotte, and Mary

Ellen. They were no longer among the living because of her.

"Babe, don't do it," Clayton whispered in her ear. "Don't let the enemy in your head."

She nodded. "You get changed. I'm going to see what I can come up with for lunch."

"Are you okay?"

She met his gaze. "I'll be fine. How about you?"

Clayton kissed her. "Why don't you come upstairs with me? We can relax in that Jacuzzi tub like we used to do—it's been a while since we've done that."

"I guess lunch can wait."

Chapter 19

SMILING, Natalia eyed her computer monitor as she clicked print.

Her printer began spitting out flyers she'd spent the morning working on—they were perfect for what she had in mind.

Natalia grabbed her purse as soon as the printing was completed.

"It's about to get real for you, Jessica."

Chapter 20

JESSICA WALKED TO THE MAILBOX. As she neared it, she saw a flyer hanging from it. From another lawn or house cleaning service, she surmised.

She waved at her neighbor, but the woman did not wave back, which was unusual. Jessica saw her looking at the flyer, then at her.

Jessica noticed the picture on the paper first. It was of her. Horrified, she snatched it up. Someone had distributed flyers in her neighborhood with her photo and the word murderer.

"Jessica..."

She looked up and saw Clayton jogging toward her. He had a stack of papers in his hand. He must have found them posted along the route he usually took on his daily run.

He slowed the jog to a walk as he neared her. Without uttering a word, Clayton gathered her into his arms, and held on. Long seconds passed as they clung together, each taking strength from the other.

Her head fell heavily against his shoulder.

"I'm sorry about this, babe. I wish there was something I could do."

She stiffened, then let out a breath. "Just hold me."

It was in that moment, Jessica felt closer to him than she ever had. She swallowed the tears gathering in the back of her throat.

Clayton ushered her into the house.

"Natalia did this," Jessica said. "This was nobody but her." She spat out the words contemptuously. "She wants to destroy every ounce of peace I have."

"I know you wanted me to stay out of this, but I've had enough.

Jessica knew that Clayton's temper when crossed could be almost uncontrollable. "Bae, we have to let it go."

"No, we are not." The angry retort hardened his features. "I'm not going to stand by and let her harass you like this."

"This is where I live. Janice wouldn't even speak earlier. Now all of our neighbors know about me."

"We can always sell the house," Clayton suggested. "I probably should have done that in the first place."

"It wouldn't have mattered. Natalia would have found out where we lived. The only way to not have to deal with her is to move away."

"Why don't we go to a hotel for a few days?"

Jessica nodded. "Lock ourselves away and order room

service? Yes, I think I'd like that. Right now, I'd rather be anywhere but here."

Chapter 21

DEAN STROLLED into the restaurant looking courtroom fresh. When he spotted Clayton, he headed in his direction. "I'm not sure why you wanted to meet, but I assume it has to do with my wife and yours."

"It definitely has to do with your wife, Dean. She's been harassing Jessica and if you can't make her stop, I'm going to have my lawyer petition the court for a restraining order. We will also file a formal charge of harassment against Natalia. My wife has served her time and is simply trying to move forward—she doesn't need to be humiliated in restaurants or come home to posters like this plastered all over our neighborhood." Clayton handed the flyer to Dean.

"What makes you think Natalia would do something like this?" he asked. "She wasn't your wife's only victim."

"One of my neighbors saw her and took pictures. You're an attorney. You know this isn't right."

"It's funny hearing you talk about what's right. I'm

pretty sure you had a hand in trying to frame my wife for the murders committed by Jessica, although it was never proven. Do you think it was right to try and send my wife to prison for something she didn't do?"

Irked by Dean's cool, aloof manner, but Clayton did not react. "I have proof that your wife is harassing *my* wife. I came to you as a man asking that you tell Natalia to cease and desist. If she doesn't, then I will be forced to take legal action, which includes sending a letter to the American Bar Association."

Dean clenched his mouth tighter. "My wife went through a lot because of Jessica."

"No one is excusing that. My wife went to prison and justice was served."

"That's the problem—Natalia doesn't think it was..."

"That's *her* problem, Dean. That is something you two must deal with. The law says that my wife served her time and is free to move forward with her life."

Dean stiffened, his vexation clear. "I'll talk to her."

"That's all I'm asking. I want you to know that I'm not unsympathetic to what Natalia's gone through. Jessica and I weren't together then, but I'd like to think that had we been together—none of us would be in this space right now."

A waiter came over to their table.

"Just water please," Dean said.

"Same but with lemon." Clayton picked up his menu. "Lunch is on me."

"You don't have to—"

"I invited you and I'm a man of my word."

"I heard about your sermon. A friend of mine attends Bright Hope and he said that he really enjoyed your message."

"To God be the glory," Clayton said.

Dean studied him openly. "I have to confess that I didn't believe that you'd made the huge transformation, but looking at you right now, and from everything I've heard... it's true."

"People can change."

The waiter brought their waters, then took food orders.

"How is Jessica?" Dean asked.

"She's fine," Clayton said. "My wife just wants to move forward. She's not looking to hurt anyone."

"That's good to hear."

Clayton and Dean remained civil as they ate their lunch.

"Thank you."

"It was my pleasure, Dean."

They shook hands.

"I appreciate you coming to me, man to man."

Clayton gave a slight nod, then walked toward his car. He hoped Dean would be able to get Natalia to back off. He and Jessica wanted to avoid unwanted attention. While they were at the hotel, she had even suggested they leave town. The fact that Jessica would even consider leaving her family—this thing with Natalia was taking its toll on her.

"HEY HONEY," Natalia said when Dean entered her office.

"What were you thinking?" he asked, holding up the flyer. His voice filled with a vague hint of disapproval.

She settled back in her chair, arms folded across her chest. "Where did you get that?"

"Are you denying that you put these up in the neighborhood where Jessica lives?"

"I'm not denying anything," Natalia responded. "I simply want to know how you ended up with one of them."

"I just left Clayton," Dean said. "He wanted to warn me that if I'm not able to rein you in—he's going to file harassment charges against you, obtain a restraining order, and file a complaint with the Bar Association."

"He's got some nerve..." she uttered, her lips puckered in annoyance.

"*He has every right*," Dean stated, "It looks like you're stalking his wife. We've worked too hard building our law firm and our reputation, Natalia. Surely, you realize that this could become problematic if you don't stop."

"He can't prove I put those flyers out."

"Yes, he can," Dean said. "One of his neighbors has you on camera."

"It doesn't matter. She's the criminal. I felt her neighbors needed to know who's living in their community."

"Did you give them a list of sexual predators, too? Oh, and what about the shoplifters?"

"I get your point, Dean."

"Are you willing to risk your career over this vendetta? Jessica has rights just like you and I." He sat down in one of the chairs facing her desk. "Let's talk about this on a spiritual level."

Natalia sighed. "Here we go..."

"Really?"

"I know what you're going to say, Dean. *Sin is sin.* Well, if Jessica is going to heaven, then I don't want to be there."

It was clear that her words troubled him.

"How can you claim to be a Christian and hold that viewpoint?" Dean wanted to know. "I don't understand it. Is there no joy in knowing that a sinner has turned to God? More importantly, isn't Christ's blood enough to make even the vilest offender clean and acceptable to the Father? Don't forget that Moses and David were both murderers, but the Bible tells us of the great works

God did in their lives."

"So, you really believe that Jessica has changed? She has a mental illness—that's why the judge gave her some leniency in her sentence. Well... she hasn't been cured. She could easily lose it again."

"Then again, she may not," he countered. "The truth is that we are all candidates for murder and mayhem. It doesn't take someone mentally ill or even an evil person to do such things. I believe we are all capable of everything she did, if we didn't have God in our lives."

"I just struggle with the idea that God's grace covers any and every sin." Natalia looked at Dean. "It's hard for me to believe that sociopaths can change. That's one of the reasons I never went into criminal law."

"I guess you have to remember that none of us deserves

God's forgiveness and salvation, sweetheart. The Bible says we all have sinned, and we all deserve only God's judgment. But the good news is that God loves us, and Christ came into the world to save us. When we repent of our sins and receive Him into our hearts, God has promised to forgive us—completely and fully. This includes Jessica. You don't know what's in her heart."

"I'm glad y'all can find it so easy to just forgive her, but I can't." Natalia picked up a stack of documents on her desk. "I need to get back to work."

Dean walked toward the door, pausing long enough to say, "Just promise me that you'll stay away from Jessica."

"I don't want to be in the same room with her."

When her husband left, Natalia leaned back in her chair, a grin on her face. *Poor Jessica. Had to have her hubby come fight her battle. It's not over. This is just the beginning.*

Chapter 22

"WHERE HAVE YOU BEEN?" Jessica asked. "I took a nap and when I woke up, you were gone."

"I had lunch with Dean Anderson."

"Why?" she inquired, following him into the family room.

"I told him about the flyers and that I want the harassment to stop," Clayton said.

Jessica did not respond right away. After a moment, she stated, "Bae, I appreciate what you did, but I really didn't want you to get involved."

"You're my wife and I'm not just going to stand by while this woman tries to make your life miserable. It's not right and I could tell that Dean wasn't pleased by this at all."

"You know that you've just declared war against them, right?"

"I don't think so," Clayton said. "I met with Dean man

to man and I wasn't disrespectful. I prayed before I even called him. He heard me out and then we had lunch. I did the right thing—I just want him to do the same. Talk to his wife and get her to leave you alone."

Jessica walked toward him, then winced.

"What happened?"

"I thought I'd run today, but I got a cramp or something before I was two doors down. I guess it's because I'm out of practice."

Clayton sat down on the sofa and motioned for her to join him. He pulled her leg into his lap, then began to massage it, up and down her calf with just a light pressure.

"You're so good to me."

"Jessica, I love you."

Her heart turned over in response. "I love you, too."

Clayton stopped manipulating her calf and in a swift, fluid movement slid closer to her, close enough that he leaned forward and pressed his lips to hers.

Jessica responded by leaning forward slightly as their kiss grew deeper.

"Too bad you've already taken that nap."

"I doubt we'd get much sleep anyway," she told him. "Besides, you need to prepare for Bible Study. You're teaching tonight, right?"

"Yeah. I know what I'm going to teach on. I already have my notes ready."

Jessica gave him a sidelong glance. "I still can't get over how much you've changed. I'm happy about it, don't get me wrong. I just remember when I told you that I was

giving my life to Christ and that expression on your face—
you looked horrified."

"All I could think about was that you were going to be
another Jesus Junkie and I didn't want any parts of it."

"Which surprises me," Jessica said. "You talked about
how much you enjoyed Vacation Bible School and
learning about God."

"What I didn't say was that when I was 24, I was ready
to give my life to the Lord. I went to this church on the
corner. When I walked inside, the first person I saw was
one of my best customers—he was the preacher."

"Are you serious?"

Clayton nodded. "I just turned around and walked
out. I can't even explain the disappointment I felt. After
you told me about that guy you were seeing who was
stealing money from his church..."

"Michael Jennings," she interjected.

"I figured all preachers were hypocrites until I got to
know Traynor, your brother and Chrissy. These are the
only ministers I've ever met who actually live what they
preach about. One thing I never wanted to do—I never
wanted to say one thing and do another. I didn't want to
become a preacher if I couldn't live up to the hype."

"I feel the same way," Jessica stated, "I want to get a
degree and go to seminary. I feel like I need to have creden-
tials, so people will take me seriously. I don't want people
to think I'm a fraud or that I'm trying to get over on innocent people. I've already got enough stuff working against
me. I'm a murderer and ex-con..."

"That's who you used to be, babe. That's not you anymore."

"Thank you for believing in me."

His hand took her face and held it gently. "Thank God for second chances."

Chapter 23

"TWINS..." Chrissy glanced over at her husband. "We're having two babies." She was experiencing some pain on her left side, so her doctor recommended they come in to ensure the pregnancy wasn't ectopic.

"I'm speechless," Aiden uttered, complete surprise on his face. "We're definitely going to have our hands full with four children."

"I'm up to the challenge," she responded with a grin. "I guess we shouldn't be so stunned about this. I'm a twin."

"You're a fraternal twin, so the chances of you having twins is as many as 1 in 7," her doctor explained. "Another fact is that the chance of giving birth to twins or multiples increases as a woman ages. Almost 20% of births among women over 40 were twins."

Chrissy looked at the monitor of the ultrasound. "Our babies are fraternal twins."

"Yes," her doctor confirmed. "Each twin has his or her own placenta and amniotic sac."

"In terms of prenatal care, what changes now that we know that I'm carrying twins?"

"As you know, taking care of yourself is the best way to take care of your babies. This means more frequent checkups, ultrasounds, or other tests, especially as your pregnancy progresses. There is a possibility of an earlier delivery."

They were still in a daze when they left the doctor's office.

"I'm relieved it wasn't an ectopic pregnancy," Chrissy said when they were in the car heading home.

Aiden agreed. "I'm thankful everything looks normal."

Chrissy looked out the passenger side window. "There was a time when I didn't believe I would ever have the life I have with you. I'm really a testimony that your beginning does not have to be your ending." Tears slipped from her eyes and down her cheek. "God has been so good to me... to us..."

"He sure has," Aiden said. "I can't thank Him enough."

Chrissy wiped her face with a tissue.

"You okay, babe?"

"I'm feeling a bit overwhelmed right now, but in a good way." She glanced outside the window once more. It's such a pretty day. Do you have to go back to work?"

"No, I don't have to," he responded. "What's up?"

"Why don't we take the kids to lunch and afterward, we can stop by the park. It's too nice to stay inside today."

Smiling, Aiden said, "I can't think of anything I'd like to do more than spend time with my wife and children."

Chrissy reached over and gave his right hand a gentle squeeze. "Thank you."

Chapter 24

"HEY, THIS IS A PLEASANT SURPRISE," Jessica said when she opened the front door to find Holt standing there. "If I'd known you were coming by, I would've prepared something to eat."

"I'm good," he responded. "Clayton told me what's been going on and I just wanted to check on you."

"I'm doing okay. You don't have to worry about me."

"I'm sorry you have to deal with a woman who's so hungry for revenge. Eventually, she'll grow bored and it will be on to the next person."

"After everything I've done to Natalia—it's just hard to see her as vindictive. She's giving me back what I gave her."

Holt smiled. "Jessica, I want you to know that I'm very proud of you and the way you've handled yourself."

"Being on probation is a great motivator," she confessed with a grin. "I have to tell you... there are times when I want to get in my flesh, but Clayton keeps me grounded as well. I still can't get over how much he's changed. He is truly a new creature in Christ."

"I witnessed firsthand his transformation. I was at the church the day he came by to talk to my dad. He looked at us, then said he was tired of running. Then he just broke down into sobs." Holt paused a moment, then said, "Clayton got himself together, then told us that he wanted to change his life—he said that God had been dealing with him for years, but he would just run."

Jessica nodded. "He told me once that God had called him to preach and I remember laughing. I think I hurt his feelings because he never mentioned it again. When he talked about going to Vacation Bible School in his sermon —that was the first time I'd heard about that."

"He ran because he didn't feel worthy—he felt God couldn't use a *tainted* man, as he put it. That's when my father took him to the Bible. Dad told him about David, Moses, Jonah—he showed Clayton how God uses flawed people to show there is still hope in a flawed world. Clayton was the first to arrive on Sunday mornings and he never missed a Bible study. We could set our clocks by him." He laughed. "We still can."

Jessica chuckled. "That's my bae. He doesn't like to be late to anything. I'm so grateful to you and Traynor for helping him find his way. When I told Clayton I was ready to give my life to the Lord, I didn't think we'd stay together. I knew that I couldn't stay with him unless he changed his life, and I couldn't force him to do that."

"But God..." Holt said with a smile. "Look at the two of you now."

"I have an appointment with my therapist tomorrow," Jessica announced. "I went with the woman Angela recommended."

"That's good."

"Clayton and I have decided to sell this house. We're actually thinking about moving to another state—not too far away. It will be good for us and for Natalia."

"Really?"

She nodded. "I'm actually going to see Chrissy after my session tomorrow. I'm going to have her list it for sale. I just think it's for the best, but it's not an immediate thing because we have to decide on where to relocate; we have to talk to my probation officer—there's a lot that has to take place first."

Chapter 25

"SO, you and Clayton really want to sell the house?"

Jessica nodded.

"Do you have any ideas where you want to buy?"

"We've talked about leaving Raleigh, Chrissy. Natalia is on a mission to ruin my life—it's only fair... after all I tried to take her life on more than one occasion."

"You've served your time. You shouldn't have to leave town. She needs to leave you alone and I'm gonna tell her just that."

"Natalia is entitled to her feelings, but I just want to move forward with my life. When I found that flyer, don't get me wrong... I was livid. I wanted to drive over to her house and wring her neck. That woman really knows how to push my buttons, so I think it's best that Clayton and I move to another city. I just hate the thought of leaving my family. We don't plan on living too far away that we can't visit often."

"There's something I have to tell you," Chrissy said.

"Aiden and I went to see the doctor because I was experiencing some pain—"

Jessica interrupted her by asking, "Is the baby okay?"

"Yes, *they're* fine," Chrissy responded with a grin.

"Oh, thank the Lo—," she stopped short. *"They're* fine? They as in multiples?"

"They as in twins. We're having twins."

Jessica's eyes grew wet. "Oh, my goodness. That's wonderful. Another set of twins in the family."

"When I first found out, I tried to picture myself in my fifties with a set of teenagers. Girl..."

"You're gonna do just fine, sis."

"I never thought I could be this happy."

Jessica nodded in agreement. "I know what you mean."

"Does it bother you that you're not able to give Clayton a child?" Chrissy asked. "It's so obvious how much you love children."

"It did at one time, but I've made my peace with it. Adoption is out of the question because of my past. I'm content with just being an auntie. I'm really happy for you."

"Well, if you move away—I'm warning you now, I'll be sending these children to you for summer vacation."

"Don't play with me, Chrissy. You know I want visitation rights with my babies—*all* of them."

"You and Clayton are gonna need a much bigger house if you intend to take on my kids and Holt's."

"You're our agent, so I expect you to find us the perfect home."

Chapter 26

WITHIN THIRTY MINUTES Sabrina was gone with the children and the evening stretched out before Natalia. "We haven't had a whole weekend to ourselves in a long time," she told Dean.

He agreed. "So, what do you want to do?"

"Table any topics that will ignite an argument."

"I can do that."

In the living room, Natalia and Dean settled on the sofa.

She grabbed the remote to turn on the television and turned to their favorite crime drama show to binge watch. For the next four hours, they lost themselves in the world of actors in life-and-death situations.

"I've been thinking that we should celebrate our wedding anniversary on a cruise. What do you think?" Natalia asked.

"A cruise to the Mediterranean."

"Yes," she agreed. "I'll call the travel agent on Monday morning."

They made a simple meal of grilled chicken and a garden salad.

"This is really nice," Natalia said. "I love our kids, but I want more of this—quality time with you."

"We've both been a bit distracted lately."

Natalia did not respond but she knew his comment was mostly directed at her. She'd been so focused on Jessica since the witch got out of prison. Although she knew the day was coming, Natalia never expected it to be so soon.

"We need to get back to having weekly date nights."

"Huh," she murmured. "I'm sorry, I didn't hear what you said."

"I was talking about date night. We should have one each week."

Natalia smiled. "I agree."

"Then let's get started," Dean said, holding up his iPhone.

Her heart swelled with the familiar music and the beats resounded in the blood that flowed through her veins.

Natalia swayed to the music. "I love this song."

Dean took her by the hand.

Together they moved their bodies to the rhythm.

As the music continued to play, Natalia raised her arms over her head, as she danced. She arched her back, arms still thrown over her head, and trusted that Dean would keep her safe.

If only she could trust him to do the same in real life.

Chapter 27

"I WAS INVITED to speak at a youth center in Philadelphia," Clayton announced. "The director reached out to Traynor and he felt I should go with him and speak. He felt my testimony would be more effective to the teens that will be in attendance."

Jessica clapped her hands in glee. "That's wonderful, bae. I wish I could go with you."

"I'll ask Holt to videotape it. He's going with us."

Jessica hated being on probation because she could not leave town without having permission. Even then, she would have to provide a full itinerary—it was easier for her to just stay in town. *Lord, I have three more years of this. I'm gonna need you to help me through it.*

▭

FRANKIE INVITED Jessica over to have dinner to watch a movie with her and the kids. They had a wonderful time.

She glanced down at her purple and yellow painted toenails, courtesy of the twins.

Jessica stretched and stifled a yawn. "I guess it's time for me to head home."

"You're more than welcome to stay here with us," Frankie offered. "I don't know how you can stay in the big house all alone. I guess I'm scary."

"Thanks, but I'd prefer my own bed. I don't sleep that well when Clayton's out of town. Being alone in the house doesn't really bother me. We have an alarm system—" Jessica stopped short. "I forgot to turn it on when I left earlier."

"Can't you do it from your phone?" Frankie asked. "We can."

"I probably could if I knew the account information. I don't want to call Clayton and have to hear a lecture."

"Make sure you install it on your phone—it's a great help."

"I will," Jessica said.

"Holt's going to go live so we can watch Clayton speak in real time."

"Technology has certainly changed a lot over the past eight years. I have to confess that the thought of being on social media scares me. Clayton suggested I build a Facebook page, but I'm not interested," Jessica stated.

"Once you start your ministry, you may want to consider it."

"Chrissy uses it for marketing her company. The few times I've been on Facebook, it just looks like most people just post their personal business—they are ranting about friends and family, boyfriends. I don't want to read about other people's issues. I have enough of my own and I'm certainly not going to post them on social media."

Frankie chuckled. "There's a lot of useful information on social media as well. You just have to know where to look."

Jessica did not mention that she'd looked to see if Natalia had a personal Facebook page. She'd found one, but because they were not *friends*, she was not able to see much. For all Jessica knew, Natalia had posted pictures of her for the world to condemn.

She shook away the thought. It did her no good to worry about things she could not control. Jessica and her therapist had talked about this in her last session.

"Frankie, I want you to know that Clayton and I have put some money aside for the children. We did the same for Chrissy's kids as well. I made a lot of money off the sale of the hair salons and the beauty supply stores. We don't have children of our own... I hope you don't mind."

"Thank you, Jessica. That's really very generous of you."

"I want them to be able to go to college without racking up a huge amount of debt. If they don't want to go to college, then they can use the money for their own businesses or whatever—it's up to you and Holt."

Frankie surveyed her face. "Family means everything to you, doesn't it?"

Jessica nodded. "It's all I've ever wanted in this world. When I lost my son... I wanted to die right along with him. He was such a beautiful baby and so perfect. Then when I had to have the hysterectomy because of fibroids and cysts —I went into a state of deep depression."

"I think you would've made a fantastic mother."

Jessica gave a tiny smile. "I'd like to think so."

"I see the way you are with my kids; with Caleb and Lenore... They're very lucky to have you and I'm glad you are a part of their lives."

"Thank you for trusting me with them, Frankie." She grabbed her purse. "Now before I get all emotional, I'm going to leave. I'll text you when I get home."

Frankie walked her to the door. "Travel safe."

"Goodnight."

Twenty minutes later, Jessica pulled into the garage, but something did not feel right. The hair on the back of her neck stood up.

She got out of the car, slowly taking in her surroundings. There was a small seed inside her that set off warning bells. Something was wrong, yet there were no strange cars parked on the street. There were a couple of people walking dogs, but they were farther down the neighborhood. Under the federal law known as the Brady Law, she was not allowed to have a gun, Taser, or any other deadly weapon.

Jessica unlocked the door and eased inside.

Her body stiffened in shock. Someone had broken into her home, ransacking it. The words *murderer*, *killer* and *guilty* were spray painted on the walls.

Jessica rushed out of the house, backed down the street and parked. She called the police.

Two police cars arrived within minutes of each other. A third showed up and parked.

She got out of her car saying, "I called you. I didn't know if anyone was still in the house so, I got in my car and parked down the street."

"Did you see anyone leave or any movement in the house?"

Jessica shook her head no. She wiped away her tears.

"You wait out here with Officer Reynolds and we'll go through and check out everything."

"Do you have any idea who would have done this?"

"No, I don't."

"Any idea why?" Officer Reynolds asked.

"I'm sure you know that I was recently released from prison. There are people in this town who don't think I deserve a second chance."

"For what its worth, ma'am. I don't think that way. You deserve the right to live your life in peace."

"Thank you for saying that."

"You mentioned that your husband is out of town. Are there any weapons in the house?"

"No," she responded. "I'm on probation, so my husband got rid of his guns. You're welcome to check."

Officer Reynolds gave her a sympathetic look. "Is there somewhere you can stay?"

"I've called my sister-in-law—I'm going to stay with her until my husband gets back. I just need to grab an overnight bag."

Chapter 28

FRANKIE SHOOK her head in confusion. "I find it hard to believe that Natalia would do something like this—this is low, even for her."

"I don't believe she's the person behind what happened—she just inspired it," Jessica said. She had finally stopped trembling. "I'm sure someone got hold to one of those flyers..."

"Have you told Clayton?"

She shook her head no. "I don't want to tell him something like this the night before he has to give a speech. He doesn't need the distraction. It's my fault anyway. I didn't set the alarm. If I had, it would've scared them away. One thing for sure—I want cameras installed."

"Could you tell if anything was missing?"

"Just small stuff. We have a hidden safe in the house and it didn't look disturbed."

"Why don't I make you a cup of tea," Frankie suggested.

"Thank you. I'd appreciate it."

Alone, Jessica broke into quiet sobs. She was trying so hard to just live a normal life, but Natalia was making it difficult for her.

There was a part of her that wanted to drive over to Natalia's house and scare her out of her wits—she did not like having to just sit on the sidelines and let someone torture her like this. She had never been that kind of person.

I just need to get her alone, she thought. *I could make her beg for her life like she did before.*

Guilt snaked down Jessica's spine. "Forgive me, Lord. I need to place this in your hands. I repent of my sinful thoughts."

Frankie returned with a steaming mug of herbal tea. "It's lemon lavender."

Jessica smiled. "Thank you for letting me stay here—I really don't think I can be alone right now."

"It's fine, sweetie."

"I'm getting angry now," Jessica confessed. "I feel like a victim and I don't like it. I guess I don't have a right to feel this way after what I've done, but I really hate feeling helpless."

"Don't you see that's what Natalia wants," Frankie said, "she wants to get you to slip up so that you'll be sent back to prison. You can't let her win."

"I won't," Jessica vowed. "I had to repent for my thoughts and feelings where she's concerned. I'm giving her over to the Lord."

"I've put towels in your bathroom. You're safe here, so get some rest."

"Frankie," Jessica called out. "Please don't tell Holt about this. I don't want Clayton to find out until he gets home."

"Speaking of," she began. "Why don't you two stay here with us while your house is being repaired, cleaned and painted?"

Jessica nodded. Deep down, she worried how Clayton was going to react when she told him what had taken place. He did not make idle threats. She knew he was going to seek legal action. Jessica did not really want to go there, because Natalia would make it a public battle. She did not want to see her name splashed across newspapers ever again. She hoped to convince her husband to just let this incident die a quiet death.

Chapter 29

"STAY OUT OF THE SYSTEM," Clayton was saying. "Living the life of a drug kingpin, is not worth it. The gangster fairytale that actors sell in movies to your generation is not real. Very few drug dealers live a lavish lifestyle and retire. They end up dead, in jail, strung out on drugs or like a friend of mine, paralyzed. Not too long ago, I lost a friend —he was killed in a deal gone bad. Trust me when I say there are many pitfalls in that lifestyle..."

They were able to watch the live video on Frankie's smart TV.

"Clayton did a fantastic job," Chrissy said before biting into her sandwich. "He reminds me of Traynor when he speaks—the difference is that he really knows how to reach an audience that most pastors may find a bit challenging."

"He's lived that life, so they will listen to him. That's why Traynor thought it best to have him speak to that group of teens. They are all ex-gangbangers." Jessica took a sip of lemonade. "He wants to have a youth center of his own one day—it's always been a dream of his."

"How is the pregnancy going?" Frankie inquired. "I had terrible morning sickness when I was pregnant with the girls."

"It's going really well," Chrissy responded, "except for the heartburn. I have a lot of that, so I've started carrying a bottle of Tums with me."

"Are you and Aiden planning on having a gender reveal party?"

"Girl no... we're trying to decide if we even want to know. We're thinking about waiting until they get here."

Jessica held up a hand. "Do we get a say in this?"

"What she said," Frankie interjected.

"Just from the expressions on your faces—I can tell that you both don't want to wait until I deliver."

"You can better prepare when you know the gender... I'm just saying." Frankie gave a slight shrug.

"Aiden and I talked about it at length. He figured if we knew the gender, we'd end up spending half as much time choosing names. He also said that everyone would drown us with pink or blue clothing. As for me, I like being surprised."

"You're going to get tired of everyone in the world asking if you know the gender of the babies," Jessica stated.

Frankie wiped her mouth with her napkin. "Chrissy, you can just respond we're definitely having two boys, two girls or a boy and a girl."

They burst into a round of laughter.

"Girl, can you imagine me saying something like that

to Mother Wilberta or Mother Hazel?" Chrissy asked with a laugh. "They'd run me out of the church."

Frankie nodded in agreement. "They sure would. Those old ladies treat all of us like children."

"I guess we are. Mother Wilberta is 89 and her sister is 87. I believe they're two years apart."

"They're sisters?" Jessica asked.

Frankie nodded. "They moved in together after Mother Hazel's husband died. Mother Wilberta had lost her husband two years prior. Those two ladies are some feisty women. They love Dad though."

"Now, I remember them," Jessica said. "They came up to Clayton after his trial sermon and said he'd done a decent job. The taller of the two asked him if he had really been a gansta."

Frankie chuckled. "That was Mother Wilberta."

"I cracked up when she leaned into him and said, "Jesus was the original gangsta. He didn't take no mess off nobody. She said all these imitation gangstas out here chasing the world, 'cause they lost."

Chrissy laughed. "Mother Wilberta better preach..."

Jessica's cell phone rang.

"It's Traynor." Answering it, she placed the call on speaker. "Hey... we're all here at Frankie's house."

"I'm glad you're not alone," he responded. "Sweetheart, something happened..."

"What's wrong?"

"We were outside with the teens at the center. Clayton's been shot—he pushed one of the boys out of the way. The police believe that this boy was the real target."

"Is he okay? Can I talk to him?"

"Not right now," Traynor said. "He's in surgery. He was shot in the chest."

"I need to be with him, but I don't know if they will let me leave town."

"Give me the number of your probation officer. I'll give him a call and see what can be worked out."

She burst into tears. "I can't lose him... I can't lose my husband."

Chapter 30

"ARE YOU OKAY?" Sabrina inquired. "You've been so quiet all morning. Do you need any help with packing up your office?"

"I'm fine, just a bit distracted." Chrissy's eyes traveled the length of her office. They were moving this weekend into a much larger building to accommodate their growing company. "You can have Janice finish packing in here."

"I can tell something's off with you. Do you want to talk about it?"

As their eyes met, Chrissy said, "Sabrina, I'd like to know where we stand."

"Excuse me?"

"Natalia is your cousin and Jessica is my sister. Where do *we* stand?"

A shadow of hurt colored Sabrina's expression. "I can't believe you even have to ask me something like this," she said. "You and I have been friends for a very long time. Natalia offered me a job and I turned it down. I love working here and I don't intend to leave unless I decide that my services are better suited somewhere else."

"I just needed to be sure. I know that we're both in difficult positions, but I don't want this to affect our friendship or work relationship. There needs to be trust between us."

"What we talk about, stays between the two of us, Chrissy. I hope that you know this."

"I just wanted to make sure that we're on the same page, Sabrina. You know I love you like a sister, but Natalia is your blood."

"I know. She constantly reminds me."

"I'm so sorry."

"Girl, it's gonna be fine. I know how to handle my cousin."

"Someone broke into Jessica's house and trashed it. They spray painted the words *killer* and *murderer* on the walls. I'm pretty sure Natalia wasn't behind it, but she put out a bunch of flyers with my sister's picture on it and she labeled her a murderer—I think someone got one of the flyers and took it to the extreme."

Sabrina looked horrified. "That's terrible. The scary part is that they had to be watching the house to know that she and Clayton wasn't home at the time."

"She's asked me to list the house. They want to sell it."

"I won't say a word to Natalia, if you're wondering," Sabrina stated. "I've never discussed Brown and Barton's business with her and I don't intend to start now."

"I want to share something else with you," Chrissy said. "I'm pregnant... with twins. For now, only you and

Patty will know. The rest of the staff will know eventually."

"I'm so happy for you. Chrissy, this is a miracle."

"I know. Aiden and I are just ecstatic. I have to admit that I'm a little nervous about having babies at 43, but I'm so grateful. To be honest, I consider this pregnancy a miracle."

"You're gonna be such a great mother—you already are. Caleb and Lenore are perfect children as far as I can tell. They are so well-behaved and respectful. Natalia's children... I love them, but they are so spoiled. And Minx—that little girl is something else. She has her mother's temper."

"They're so cute," Chrissy said. "It's hard to keep from spoiling them when they're little, but if you're not careful, they may make you pay for it when they're older."

"Back to you, so how far along are you?"

"Eleven weeks. And before you ask, we are going to wait until they're born to find out the gender. We want to be surprised."

"I can respect that," Sabrina said. "I don't need to be pushy, but you still look like something's weighing heavy on your mind."

"Clayton was in Philadelphia this weekend to speak at a youth center. There was a drive-by and he was shot in the chest. He was outside the place talking to a young man. With no thought for his own life, Clayton pushed him out of the way—the teen was the target."

"Is he okay? I know Jessica must be beside herself."

"He's doing fine. They were able to remove the bullet.

He'll be in the hospital a few more days. I still can't get over the fact that Clayton risked his own life to save that boy."

"That was very heroic."

"Traynor said when Clayton was conscious, he kept asking if the boy was okay. He and Holt went with him to Philly." Chrissy intentionally left out the fact that Jessica was at the hospital with her husband. She did not want to risk Sabrina letting it slip to Natalia, even though her sister had obtained permission to travel out of state from her probation officer.

"I'll keep Clayton in my prayers."

The topic turned to what needed to be done to make the company relocation a smooth one.

Chapter 31

"HEY YOU," Jessica murmured when Clayton opened his eyes. "How are you feeling?"

"S-sore," he managed. "I thought I dreamed you."

She stroked his cheek. "I'm real, baby. I'm really here. It's not a dream."

"How?"

"Traynor spoke with my probation officer—She gave me permission to leave. I have to check in with her as soon as we get back to Raleigh though. I was so afraid that I was going to lose you. What were you thinking?"

"I had to save that b-boy."

"I'm proud of you, but you do realize that you could have died?"

"I don't mind dying for a good cause, babe." He shifted his body and winced at the pain. "I know that's hard for you to hear."

"I don't want to live without you, Clayton." A lone tear slipped from her eye. "I never realized just how much I love you until Traynor called and told me that you'd been shot. I hadn't realized until then just how much you are a part of me."

"Please don't cry."

"I'm sorry. I know you're not used to seeing me so emotional, but I seem to be all over the place lately."

"You've been through a lot. I didn't mean to add to it, but I couldn't just stand by and watch that boy die."

"When I first heard that you had been shot, I thought this was my punishment—the consequence for taking someone else's life."

"Babe, you know God doesn't work that way."

"In my mind, I know it, but in my heart—I let my fear of losing you take over." Jessica took his hand in her own. "I thank God that you're going to be fine."

"I pray that young man will be safe," Clayton said. "He may need to leave Philadelphia."

Holt knocked on the half open door.

Once inside, he said, "Eric... the teen you saved, is on a bus heading to Savannah, Georgia. He's going to be living with his grandmother. The director of the center drove him and his mother to Delaware—that's where they boarded."

"Praise the Lord," Clayton said. "Thank you, Jesus."

"He wanted to come to the hospital to see you, but we didn't think it was safe, so he wrote you a letter."

"Would you please read it?"

Holt opened it up and began reading.

Pastor Clay:
I am glad to hear that you are doing good. I would feel bad if

you had died because of me. I don't want nobody to be hurt. I liked listening to you talk about your life and how you walked away from selling drugs. When my brother Carlos got killed, I saw what it did to my mama. I knew I didn't want her to go through that again, so I left that life behind. The thing is, I know stuff and even though I told them I'll keep my mouth shut. I guess they don't believe me.

Mr. Vasquez and you have shown me that there are people who still have not given up on me. I didn't know I was hurting people and that I was hurting myself, too. I want you to know that being that close to death really scared me. I want to live and make my mama proud. I hope that I can write or call you sometime. Mr. Vasquez said that he didn't think you would mind, so he gave me the number and address of your church.

Because you almost died for me, I make you a promise. I will live the life that my brother didn't have a chance to live and be good.

Eric Chastain

Handing the paper to Clayton, Holt said, "You certainly made an impression on that young man."

Jessica gently wiped away her tears. "What a beautiful letter."

"To God be the glory," her husband whispered.

Chapter 32

"SABRINA'S AT THE NEW LOCATION," Chrissy said when Natalia sashayed through the double doors.

"Oh, by the way... I heard the police were at your sister's house over the weekend. A friend of mine lives in that neighborhood. What kind of trouble did she get herself into this time?"

"It wasn't like that and if you're here to gloat, then you might as well leave," Chrissy responded, sending a sharp glare in Natalia's direction. "Better yet, *maybe* I should call the police and tell them about what you've been doing to my sister. Her house was broken into and trashed because of you."

Natalia seemed genuinely surprised by the news. "I have better things to do with my time."

"Oh, I'm sure you didn't get your manicured fingers dirty, but I know how much you hate her."

I'll admit to doing what I can to torment her, but I wouldn't go into her house."

"*Really?* Because I remember a time when you did break into her home," Chrissy said.

She remained silent for a moment, then said, "Chrissy, I don't deny that I wanted to punish her—ruin her life like she tried to ruin mine."

"From where I'm sitting, it doesn't look like your life is too bad. You have a husband who adores you, beautiful children, a successful business—how exactly is your life ruined?"

"The best thing for Jessica to do is to just disappear. I'm not going to stand still and let her manipulate people into believing she's suddenly changed for the better."

"She has a right to live wherever she chooses, Natalia. You know it wasn't that long ago when everyone was saying how you weren't a very nice person. I heard how you tried to manipulate my brother into a marriage."

"I *have* changed."

"Not as much as you'd like to think," Chrissy responded. "You still think that you're so much better than other people. You're still the same judgmental and vindictive person that you've always been."

"You have a right to your beliefs just as I have a right to mind," Natalia said before storming out of the office.

Chapter 33

"CLAYTON and I want to leave Raleigh," Jessica announced to her family when they came over to the house for a visit. Her husband was released after a week in the hospital. They stayed an additional two days before flying home. She was grateful to them for making sure the house had been put back in a livable state.

"After everything that's happened, Clayton and I feel it's best that we start our ministry far away from here."

"Where will you go?" Traynor asked.

"We haven't decided on that," she responded truthfully.

"The reason I ask is because I may have an idea. Your grandparent's property passed to Jessie Belle and her children... I still have the house in Brookhaven as well. You can tear down or renovate the old house—I've done my best to keep it up."

Jessica looked at Holt. "That house belongs to you. Jessie Belle didn't know anything about me and Chrissy."

"I want you to have it," he said. "We have no plans on leaving North Carolina."

"At least let me pay you for it."

Holt shook his head. "You're my sister. We each have a ownership share in that property. I'm willing to sign over my share to you."

"So am I," Chrissy said.

"The old church is there as well," Traynor interjected. "It's been closed for years, so it'll need a little work, but I think it's a good place to start your ministry."

"Sis, you're really considering this?"

Jessica nodded. "Chrissy, I don't have a choice. I just want to move forward with what God has called me to do. I've prayed about this... Clayton and I believe that leaving is the best thing—at least it might give Natalia some peace. I spoke to my probation officer and we can leave if whatever state—in this case, Georgia, agrees to the transfer."

"There's a correctional facility for youth not too far from Mayville." Traynor said. "I think they could use someone like Clayton."

"I'll talk to him about everything, then I'll call my probation officer to find out what we need to do to get this process started."

"How are you feeling, sweetie?" Jessica inquired when Clayton opened his eyes. He'd slept through the visit from Traynor and the rest of the family.

"Tired..."

"It's time to take your medicine, but first you need to eat something. I've made you some soup and a sandwich."

"Did your family leave?"

She nodded. "They didn't want to wear you out."

Jessica sat down beside Clayton in bed. "I told them about our decision to leave Raleigh."

"How did they take it?"

"Actually, very well. In fact, Traynor offered my grand-mother's house in Georgia to us. He also said the church built by my great-grandfather is still there—sitting on the property and empty. It could be a fresh start for us—that is if Georgia accepts the transfer of my probation."

Inclining his head, Clayton asked, "You want to go back to Georgia?"

"Yeah... I think I do... maybe I need to do this—go back to where it all started." Jessica eyed him. "What about you? How do you feel about living in tiny Mayville, Georgia?"

"I'll go wherever you will feel safe and happy."

"When I left that town after Jessie Belle's funeral, I never thought I'd ever see that place again."

Clayton nodded in agreement. "Sometimes we have to face the past before we can look to the future."

Chapter 34

AFTER A SIX-HOUR DRIVE, Jessica and Clayton arrived in Mayville, Georgia.

It had taken a couple of months to get everything in order for the move, but that was all behind them now. After spending Labor Day with the family, they left early the next day.

They parked behind Mayville Baptist Church which shared the lot with a parsonage—the house that once belonged to Elias and Anabeth Holt.

Jessica knew at first glance that they were going to need to do some major renovations.

"We're definitely going to need to add a master bedroom with full bath—the works," she murmured as they toured the house. I love the hardwood floors—they just need to be refinished."

"I think we should make the two existing bedrooms a little larger," Clayton stated. "Let's put a bathroom in each one and a guest bath downstairs."

"You know we're talking about tearing this house down and rebuilding it."

He nodded. "I like the style, but it needs some serious updating. I'd like to brick it all around... the church, too. Some of that wood on the side of the church looks rotted."

"Let's tackle the house first."

Clayton agreed. "We'll meet with an architect to have some plans drawn up."

"So where are we going to live while we're rebuilding this house?"

"Traynor said we could stay in the house in Brookhaven until we get this house ready. It's not too bad— I think it just needs to be thoroughly cleaned. I'll call a cleaning service and schedule an appointment."

For the rest of the day, Jessica and Clayton cleaned the house enough for them to feel comfortable unpacking. "I haven't seen any bugs or rodents, but I definitely want pest control to come out."

"I found a couple of dead bugs. Wasn't enough to really worry about, but just to be sure—see if you can reach someone. Maybe they can come today."

Jessica chuckled. Clayton hated bugs just as much as she did. "I'm on it."

Chapter 35

JESSICA WOKE up with a smile on her face. She sat up in bed, propping a stack of pillows behind her. "That's probably the best sleep I've had in a while."

"It's probably because we're in a town where nobody knows anything about us," Clayton said. "We don't have to worry about Natalia popping up and trying to humiliate you."

"I feel like I really have a fresh start now."

He smiled. "That's good."

"Bae, how about we do some sightseeing today?" Jessica suggested with a grin.

"Sightseeing," Clayton repeated. "What is there to see in this small town?"

"Let's explore and find out."

They showered and got dressed.

Clayton and Jessica had breakfast at the Mayville Inn.

"I heard this place is black-owned," she said, "It's

owned and operated by the Shelton family. I wonder if they knew Elias and Anabeth."

"In a town this size," Clayton responded. "Probably."

She finished off her pancakes. "The food is delicious."

He agreed. "We'll have to come back here for dinner one night."

"I saw a pharmacy down the street. I need to stop there and pick up a few things." Jessica glanced over her shoulder. Her gaze locked with that of a Caucasian woman who was seated a few tables away. The woman was openly staring at her.

Probably curious because we're new in town, Jessica decided. She gave a tiny smile, then returned her attention to Clayton.

"You know, when I came here for Jessie Belle's funeral, I didn't take time to really see the town. The truth is that it wouldn't have held any appeal for me back then anyway."

Clayton agreed. "Everybody around here is so friendly."

She laughed. "It's kind of creepy, huh?"

He wiped his mouth on his napkin. "Yeah."

"Bae, we'll get used to it. In a few months, we'll probably be walking around saying *hey* and talking to everybody."

"I don't think so."

"Okay, Pastor Clay," Jessica said before laughing. "I can't wait to see you in some denim overalls."

"Now that is never happening," Clayton responded.

They left the Inn and walked down the street to Hamilton's Pharmacy.

A middle-aged man greeted them by saying, "You must be new in town. I don't think I've ever seen you in here before. I'm Wilton Hamilton, Jr. Everybody 'round here calls me Will."

Jessica nodded. "We just moved here." Her eyes traveled the store. "I don't think I've ever been to a pharmacy that wasn't in a Target or CVS. How long have you been in business?"

"Over fifty years," the man responded. "My grandfather was a pharmacist and so is my dad, although he's retired now."

"Wow, another black-owned business. I'm impressed." Jessica had no idea Mayville had so much African American history."

"The hospital here was black-owned as well, but it was sold in 2000 to some fancy corporation."

An older version of Wilton walked out of what she assumed was a stock room of some sort.

"That's my father right there. C'mere Dad." When the man ambled over, he continued, "This is Wilton Hamilton Sr."

Jessica shook the elderly man's hand. "It's really nice to meet you, Mr. Hamilton."

He pushed his glasses up his nose. "What's your name, young lady?"

"It's Jessica. Jessica Wallace. My husband and I just moved here from Raleigh."

The man adjusted his glasses. "You have family here? You look familiar to me for some reason."

"Dad, it's time for your medicine," his son interjected before she could respond.

"Well, I won't keep you," the elderly man said. "Nice meeting you both. Welcome to Mayville." He glanced at Jessica. "I'm gonna think of it. You remind me of someone."

She walked down the aisles, collecting toiletries and other necessary items.

They paid for their purchases.

Jessica smiled and slipped on her sunglasses as she navigated toward the exit doors. There were no long lines, no people rushing to and fro--everything moved at a steady but relaxed pace. Living in Mayville might not be too bad.

Chapter 36

"YOU'RE sure you ready to go inside?" Clayton asked.

Jessica nodded. "Now is just as good a time as any. We've already started renovations on the house. We need to at least see what needs to be done to the church." The first and last time she'd been in that church was when she was going by the name Reina Cannon. She had come to Mayville to attend Jessie Belle's funeral.

Dressed in an expensive designer suit, Jessica had eased into the sanctuary wearing a black hat with an attached veil made of lace to cover her face. She remembered the thrill of finding a seat on the pew behind the seating that had been reserved for the family. Jessica remembered the closed stainless-steel casket, that encased Jessie Belle's body and shuddered inwardly. Terrible regrets assailed her.

"Hon, you okay?" Clayton asked.

"I'm fine," she responded.

He unlocked the doors.

They entered the traditionally designed church which was complete with a kitchen and fellowship hall—additions Jessica was sure had been added by Elias during his leadership. Her eyes traveled the sanctuary. "I love the stain glass windows, the 30' foot ceilings with the exposed beams."

"I envision a couple of offices, a room for choir practice, and a classroom or two."

"I think we should keep the original flooring in here, too." Jessica ran her hand over a dusty pew. "We're definitely going to need some new seating in here."

"This church will hold maybe eighty people at best."

"We said we were going to start small. I think it's perfect."

Jessica walked up to the front of the church. Just as she was about to step into the pulpit, she felt a chill. She rubbed her arms up and down.

"Are you cold?" Clayton asked.

"I don't know how to explain what just happened. I just felt something go through me." Jessica glanced up at him. "I was here for Jessie Belle's funeral. I never thought I'd ever set foot back into this church again." She abandoned the idea of standing at the cross-shaped podium. "My grandfather preached up there. My maternal grandfather and great-grandfather both preached here. It was built by my great-grandfather... Jessica bit her lip until it throbbed like her pulse.

Clayton walked over and embraced her. "You feel them in here, don't you?"

She nodded. "I feel their presence. They put their

heart and soul into building their ministries. I've brought them so much shame." Jessica's eyes darkened with pain. "From this point forward, I want to honor their legacies."

"You will," he assured her. "I feel like our move here was God-ordained."

Jessica agreed. "I think so, too. It just feels right."

"HELLO MR. HAMILTON... how are you today?" Jessica inquired when she spotted him at the back of the store.

"It's a good day," he responded with a smile. "Bones don't ache as much right now."

"That's good to hear. I have to tell you... I hope to have your energy when I'm your age."

He laughed. "I try to keep moving... I'm afraid if I just sit still—I'll die."

Jessica chuckled.

"Are you related to the Grainger family? I heard you moved into the house that used to belong to Elias and Anabeth Holt. You kinda look like Agnes Grainger."

"Yes, I am," Jessica replied. "Agnes Grainger was my great-grandmother. Elias and Anabeth were my grand-parents."

He looked surprised. "They only had one child that I know of—Jessie Belle... that your mama?"

Jessica nodded. "Yes, she is."

Scratching his head, he said, "I don't remember Anabeth ever mentioning that she had a granddaughter, but then my memory ain't what it used to be."

"She actually has two daughters... I have a twin sister. We have a brother... Holt." Jessica decided not to mention that Anabeth wanted the secret of her granddaughters to die with her. A thread of anger welled up in her, but she swallowed it down.

"Now I remember her talking about the boy."

"So, you knew my grandmother."

"I loved her. She was the love of my life."

It was Jessica's turn to be surprised. "What happened... if you don't mind my asking."

"Her parents didn't think I was good enough for her. They wanted her to marry a preacher man—so she did."

"Did she feel the same way about you?"

He nodded. "Anabeth loved me as much as I loved her, but she was a good woman. She didn't want to hurt Elias. When he died, I went to her, but your grandmother sent me home. She wasn't willing to tear apart my family. She had this saying... you can't live in yesterday. Yeah... she was a good woman."

Jessica could not help but wonder how Anabeth could just throw away two helpless babes who never asked to come into this world. Poor Mr. Hamilton had been blinded by love for sure—it was obvious to Jessica that the only person Anabeth ever loved was herself.

Chapter 37

"WHAT TOOK YOU SO LONG?" Clayton asked when Jessica returned home.

"I was talking to Mr. Hamilton... he knew my grandparents--Agnes, my great-grandmother. Better yet, he and Anabeth had a thing—they were in love."

"Really?"

She nodded. "He wanted to marry Anabeth, but her parents didn't approve. They wanted her to marry Elias. After Elias passed away, Mr. Hamilton said he went to her, but she sent him away. Anabeth didn't want to break up his family, which I find funny because she sure didn't mind tearing apart her own family though." Jessica shook her head. "He had all this wonderful stuff to say about her, and all I could think about was how he didn't really know her at all."

"We all have our secrets," Clayton said.

She kissed his cheek. "There are no secrets between us and I'm glad."

"In that small bedroom closet, there is a box with pictures in it," he said. "Your grandmother... she was a beautiful woman. Oh, there's another box with a bunch of stuff in it—you should go through it."

"I'll wait until Chrissy comes down," Jessica said. "We can do it together. There may be some stuff in it that she might want to keep. Me... I'm good."

Chapter 38

IT WAS A SLOW DAY, so Chrissy was in Sabrina's office chatting. "Caleb and Lenore are very excited about the babies. Of course, Caleb's already told us that he won't be changing diapers."

They heard the door open.

Chrissy peeked out into the reception area. Turning back to face Sabrina, she said, "It's Natalia. Does she ever put in a full day at her law firm?"

Sabrina shrugged.

"Hello Natalia," Chrissy greeted.

"Hi," she responded. "I stopped by to see if my cousin wants to have lunch with me."

"I'm meeting my boo for lunch today," Sabrina said.

Chrissy sank back down in one of the empty chairs while Natalia stood in the doorway. "Can't you reschedule?"

"I could but I'm not."

Natalia looked over at Chrissy. "I heard that your sister and Clayton sold their house."

"What does that have to do with you?"

"I was just curious."

Chrissy bit back her irritation. "Why don't you mind your own business for a change? Focus on those beautiful children of yours."

"I don't need you to tell me what I should be doing. I'm a grown woman."

"And a petty one at that," Chrissy retorted.

"I also heard that Clayton's no longer on staff at Bright Hope. That was pretty short-lived."

"Natalia just stop," Sabrina said. "You should be relieved that they're gone. Now you never have to worry about Jessica. She's out of your life."

"So, they did leave town then?"

Chrissy did not respond and neither did Sabrina.

"I'll never stop looking over my shoulder as long as that woman is alive. This is what she's done to me—turned me into a woman who is afraid to leave the house at times. I still jump at unexpected noises, I'm afraid to let my children out of my sight. I intend to make sure Jessica pays for all of it."

"Natalia, I think you need to talk to a therapist," Sabrina suggested.

Chrissy rose to her feet. "I'll leave you two to finish this discussion in private."

After she left, Natalia sat down saying, "Dean has been after me to do that—see someone. He acts like I have PTSD or something."

"Maybe you do. Don't you think it is worth finding out? Make an appointment to see someone?"

"I don't want to go bare my soul to a stranger. Besides, it won't matter. As long as Jessica is alive, I will never have peace of mind."

"God can give you what you need, Natalia. But you have to let Him in."

"Sabrina, I know that. I'm just so angry. Why did He let Jessica out of prison? She should've served her full time."

"And if she had—would you be satisfied?" Sabrina questioned. "You wouldn't. Natalia. I know you."

"Maybe if Jessica had gotten the death penalty."

"So, you don't think she deserves a second chance?"

"I don't. I think she should die."

Chapter 39

CHRISSY and her family spent Thanksgiving in Mayville with Jessica and Clayton. The next day, Jessica sat in the family room while Clayton and Aiden were outside with the kids.

"How do you feel about being here?" Chrissy asked.

"It was strange at first," Jessica responded. "The woman who lived here is the one who kept us from our mother, but with all the renovations—it's pretty much a new house now."

"Sometimes, I wonder if she ever once regretted her actions."

Shaking her head, Jessica said, "Women like that—they have no regrets, Chrissy. They only care about themselves. Look at Jessie Belle. From everything we've learned, she was just like her mother."

"I wish we knew more about Anabeth."

"Why?" Jessica asked. "Do you think you can ever fully understand why she did what she did?"

"No, but it may help us find closure."

Jessica shrugged in nonchalance. "I'm good."

Chrissy's eyes caught and held hers. "Jess, are you really?"

"There will always be a thread of hurt residing in my heart. I just won't let it take over—not like before."

"Have you had any more dreams?"

"Some, but just fleeting images. Nothing like the ones where she came to talk. What about you?"

Chrissy took a sip of water. "Nothing. When she came to me that night, I think it gave some closure."

"There are some boxes that belonged to Anabeth and Elias. I guess we should go through them. Clayton found them in one of the closets. I wanted to wait on you before opening them."

"There's no time like the present," Chrissy murmured.

"I put them in the office."

Jessica led the way down the hall.

"Y'all did a nice job with the renovations. This doesn't even look like the same house."

"Thank you. It's not as big as what we had, but I'm loving it."

"I'm amazed that you were able to add two more bedrooms, an office and a sunroom."

"We took the two existing bedrooms and combined them into the master bedroom, walk-in closet and bath."

"The final renovation was completed a couple of weeks ago," Jessica said. "I wasn't sure everything would be completed by Thanksgiving, but they did it."

"I can't wait to see the church when it's finished."

Jessica and Chrissy settled on the sofa in the office. "That's it," she said, pointing to the box on the coffee table.

Chrissy opened it and pulled out a photograph. "Anabeth was very beautiful."

Jessica nodded. "Yeah, she was."

Chrissy retrieved another photograph. "Jessie Belle when she was a little girl. She looked so innocent." She released a short laugh. "We probably looked like that as well."

"I think all children look like angels at that age. But then life's trials and tribulations takes place, changing them for better or worse."

"I agree."

"Anabeth's diary," Jessica said, taking out a thick, leather bound book. "There's a couple of them in here."

"We should read them... to get some insight on our grandmother."

"Chrissy, you can read them. "I'm not ready."

"You sure? You can take one... we can read then exchange."

Jessica shook her head. "I can't right now."

"I was never one to keep a diary," Chrissy said. "All of you have that in common."

"Had... I don't have one anymore. I have a prayer and praise journal. Instead of keeping a list of the pain and hurts, I now keep a list of answered prayers."

"I think that's wonderful."

They went through the two boxes.

"Let's grab some lunch," Jessica said. "Then we can

come back and divide up this stuff. I'm sure Holt will want to have some tangible memories of Anabeth."

"You ladies, go," Clayton said. "Aiden and I will make sandwiches from the leftover ham and turkey for the kids. We're going to take them to the park in Brookhaven."

Aiden agreed. "Do your twin thing. I know how much you've missed Jessica."

Walking to the car, Chrissy said, "Girl, I love me some him."

"Yeah, I love my bae. All the hell we been through... it's worth what Clayton and I have now."

"Now that will preach, sis."

Inside the diner, Jessica felt the tiny hairs on her arm stand to attention. Her eyes slowly traveled the room, landing on a woman, she had seen a few times at the pharmacy and grocery store.

She smiled and waved.

Jessica was surprised when the woman got up and was heading toward them.

"Are you okay?" Chrissy asked.

"Don't look, but this white woman is coming over here," she said in a loud whisper.

"Do you know her?"

When the woman approached, she said, "You look just like your mother. You're Jessie Belle Holt's daughters... both of you."

Chrissy wiped her mouth with the edge of her napkin. "You knew her?"

"Everybody knows everybody," Jessica muttered. "This town isn't very big."

The woman looked at her and said, "All those whispers and rumors was true."

Chrissy glanced over at Jessica, then back at the woman. "I'm afraid we don't know what you're talking about?"

Jessica gestured for the woman to join them. "Please sit down." She was curious as to why this woman had come over to talk to them, and of what she knew about Jessie Belle. Could they have possibly been friends?

"What do you know of your father?"

"Nothing really," Chrissy said with a shrug. "Just that his name was Kenneth Walker."

"My name is Margaret Walker. He prefers to go by his middle name... Brockton."

When she got over her shock, Jessica said, "I'm Jessica and this is my sister Chrissy. I have to say that you don't look old enough to be his mother. Were you his wife?"

"He's my brother," she announced. "I'd heard all the rumors about him and Jessie Belle—even the ones about her being pregnant. I didn't really believe them until now."

Jessica laid down her fork. "So, you're our Aunt?"

Margaret nodded. "When I first saw you at the Inn, I had some suspicions, but your green eyes... I just figured you were a relative of Jessie Belle. But now looking at the two of you—I figured you must be sisters."

"I actually had my eye color changed," Jessica said. "These are implants. My eyes were the same color as my sister's—we're twins."

If Margaret was shocked by her words, she hid it well.

"Twins," she murmured. "Brockton and I are twins."

Jessica did not bother to hide her surprise. "Oh wow..."

"I often wondered if our being twins was just random, but now I see that it's more genetic," Chrissy said. "I'm pregnant with twins."

Margaret broke into a beautiful smile. "How delightful. I can't tell you how happy I am to meet you girls. Jessica, I wanted to say something to you the first day I saw you, but I wanted to be sure."

"I understand."

"I want you to know that Brockton cared for Jessie Belle. But there was no way they could ever be together— my parents never would have allowed it. Times were different than they are today."

"Did he tell you that?" Chrissy asked.

"Yes," she responded. "I confronted him when people started to whisper about them."

"Were you close to your brother?" Jessica wanted to know.

"Yes... we have always been close. We still are..."

Jessica met her sister's gaze, noting the look of shock that mirrored her own. "He's *alive?*"

Margaret nodded. "He and his family live in Atlanta."

Chrissy took a sip of her tea. "I don't know why, but I thought he was dead."

"So, did I."

"He's very much alive and he was a gifted athlete," Margaret said with a smile. "Brockton loved playing football more than anything else in life. He had a passion for it. He played in the NFL for twelve years before retiring."

"So, your brother is alive and well..." Jessica began,

"why are you telling us this? He has a family—he knows nothing about us. This is all for what?"

"I think Brockton needs to know that he has two daughters he's never met. I know my brother. He'd want to know about you."

"I find that a little hard to believe, especially since he didn't hang around after Jessie Belle told him she was pregnant," Jessica said, "He went to California and never once looked back." Shrugging, she added, "I'm sorry, but that doesn't shout *I want to be in my children's life*."

"Did she tell you this?"

"No, she wrote about it in her journals," Chrissy responded. "I think she really loved him at the time."

"Brockton had the opportunity of his lifetime—that's why he left. He had hoped to come back for her, but by the time he was ready to do it—she had gotten married. My brother and I had a huge fight about his decision. I knew it would break our parent's heart, but he didn't care—he wanted to be with Jessie Belle."

"Well, maybe that was true, but he's since gotten married and has a family. What makes you think that your brother would be remotely interested in my sister and I now?" Chrissy inquired.

"Because I know him. Brockton would at least want to meet you." Margaret shifted in her chair. "Would you be interested in meeting him? He's coming for a visit this weekend."

"I can't speak for Chrissy, but I need to think about this."

"I agree with Jessica. My sister and I have had to

process a lot since finding out that Jessie Belle was our mother—a lot has happened and not all of it good."

"I understand. Do you mind if I tell Brockton about you?"

"Will you respect our wishes if we decide that we don't want your brother to know we exist?" Jessica asked.

A flash of sadness colored her expression. "Yes, of course, but I have to confess that I want you to get to know you as well. The same blood flows through our veins. Regardless of everything that has taken place—the truth is that you are a part of my family. Outside of Brockton and his other children, you two are all that I have left."

Chrissy smiled. "Thank you for saying this, but it's a lot for us to take in right now. Here is my card... give me a call later today."

"Thank you for hearing me out."

"I'm really glad to have met you," Jessica said. "I know we're going to see each other around town—I'm open to building a relationship with you. Just not sure about the family bit just yet."

Margaret smiled. "I can respect that."

Chapter 40

"WHAT ARE YOU THINKING?" Chrissy asked when they were in the car heading home.

"Girl, I never saw that coming at all," Jessica confessed. "Like you, I thought the man was long dead. I never once thought about Googling him."

"Me either. I was so focused on Jessie Belle. I've heard of Brockton Walker—the football player. I think he did some coaching at a college when he left the NFL. I never connected *him* to Jessie Belle."

"Do you think it was because he was white?"

Chrissy shrugged. "Maybe. Maybe we thought he was far from our reach."

Jessica gave her sister a sidelong glance. "Do you want to meet him?"

"Do you?" Chrissy responded.

"I don't know. We should talk to our husbands about this. They can help us decide this next move. I don't need any emotional upheavals—I've had enough for a lifetime."

"We need to talk to you guys," Jessica said when Clayton and Aiden walked through the front door a couple of hours later.

They all settled down in the living room.

"While Chrissy and I were at the diner, we ran into a woman... her name is Margaret Walker. She is our aunt."

"She is our father's twin sister," Chrissy interjected. "Kenneth Brockton Walker is alive and living in Atlanta. He's coming to Mayville this weekend and she wants us to meet him."

"How do you feel about that?" Aiden inquired.

Chrissy glanced over at her sister. "I think Jessica and I are both conflicted. Our meeting

Jessie Belle went left with a quickness. Neither one of us want to experience that again."

"Jessica, when you brought the idea of moving here to me—the first thing that hit my spirit is that we needed to do this for you," Clayton said. "It was here in this town that you would find your peace. That you would get closure."

"Why didn't you tell me?"

"God hadn't released me to do so until now."

"After everything that's happened, I think you both should meet your father. Especially if he's open to it," Aiden said.

Chrissy looked at Jessica. "I guess we're meeting Daddy."

Chapter 41

JESSICA AND CHRISSY walked up the steps of a stately brick home with a well-maintained lawn. There were rose bushes planted neatly on both sides of the doorway.

"The flowers are beautiful," Chrissy said. "I love roses."

"I bet Margaret spends hours out here pruning them." Jessica paused to smell one of the fragrant flowers. "She looks like the type of woman who would enjoy working in the yard."

Chrissy laughed. "Are you really stopping to smell the roses? You are such a cliché. C'mon girl. Stop stalling."

"You're not the least bit nervous about meeting this man?"

"Not really," Chrissy responded. "I'd like to know more about this side of my family, especially because I'm pregnant. I want to know their medical history because it could affect my babies. I'm not looking for a daddy anymore, but if he wants to be a part of my life, then I'm open to it."

"I see your point and I agree with it."

"Jessica, you and I have a wonderful family. We have Traynor if we need fatherly advice, so it doesn't matter if Kenneth Brockton Walker accepts us or not. We're good either way."

The front door opened.

Margaret ushered them inside. "I'm so glad you two agreed to come over. Brockton is so excited about meeting you."

Family photos dotted the walls. Jessica walked slowly, taking in each one. There were photos of her father playing football. Photos of Margaret in college, graduating and of her in a wedding dress.

Brockton was seated in what looked to be a formal living room. He stood up immediately when they entered.

Margaret made the introductions.

"I'm speechless," he said. "I didn't know... Jessie Belle told me that her parents would never let her keep our baby. Her mother forced her to have an abortion with the first pregnancy. She wanted us to run away together."

"We know about all of that," Chrissy said. "She kept detailed journals. If Anabeth had had her way—my sister and I wouldn't be here either. Jessie Belle hid her pregnancy for as long as she could."

"I wanted to marry her," Brockton said, "but I was too late."

"She had a good life with Traynor," Jessica interjected. "He adored her."

"I'm glad."

"Looks like your life turned out well." Chrissy smiled. "You have a family of your own and you were able to live your dream of playing football in the NFL."

"I knew at the age of ten that I wanted to play. I made it my goal to play professionally."

"I have to confess that I'm surprised you were interested in meeting us," Jessica said.

"Family has always been important to me," Brockton responded. "I lost your mother because I didn't want to hurt my parents or lose their love. Family can be your strength, or they can be your weakness. The moment Margaret told me that she'd met you two—I cried. When Jessie Belle told me she was pregnant, I was thrilled. I wanted *my* children. I loved you and it hurt to think of what would happen when your grandmother found out. I was young, and I felt powerless. Looking back, I should have just run away with your mother. We would have been a family."

"Your life might have turned out very different," Chrissy said. "We found some of Anabeth's diaries. I started reading one of them. She never told her husband about the pregnancies because she feared it would break Elias's heart—he adored Jessie Belle. She was also worried that her daughter's actions would taint his ministry. From the entries, I read, Anabeth's heart was heavy with the weight of her secrets. She never got over the guilt."

"I can imagine the burden of such guilt," Margaret said. "If you and Jessica had opted to remain a secret—I would have had to carry that same burden within my heart."

"Secrets have a way of weighing you down," Jessica said. She had not realized that she'd said the words aloud until she saw Chrissy's expression. "I know from firsthand experience."

Margaret stood up and said, "I made some lunch. I hope you'll consider joining us."

"Sure," Jessica and Chrissy responded in unison.

———

"HE SEEMS PRETTY GENUINE," Chrissy said when they returned to the house.

Jessica agreed. "He looked really excited when you told him about Caleb, Lenore and the babies."

"I believe he really loved Jessie Belle."

"It never would've worked out for them," Jessica said. "I think she would've ruined it somehow. She really loved Traynor, but she just couldn't be the type of wife he deserved—not until after the fall."

"I guess we all have to have some kind of fall before we get ourselves together," Chrissy murmured.

"You're right about that." Jessica glanced over at her sister. "Do you really believe that Anabeth was regretful?"

"I do. People usually don't write down lies in their journals. They write what they can't share with the world or the people they love."

"I wonder why Jessie Belle didn't read them."

"The woman I knew would have hired someone to come pack up this house. I can't see her doing it herself. After Elias died, Anabeth moved to Atlanta to care for her brother Zeke. He was gay and died due to complications of AIDS."

"I'm surprised she wasn't worried about her precious reputation," Jessica uttered.

"Oh, she was," Chrissy responded. "They were estranged for a while because of it, but when she found out he was sick—she took care of him. Anabeth had cancer when she died—she never told Jessie Belle. She didn't want to disrupt her life—Holt was a senior in high school at the time."

She paused for a heartbeat, then said, "There's one part where she wrote how she tried her best to raise Jessie Belle the right way, but that she had a mind of her own—Anabeth even acknowledged that taking Jessie Belle to Gloria to get rid of us was what she thought was the best decision at the time, but she died believing that she was never more wrong. This is why I believe she regretted her actions. I really think you need to read her journals, Jess. I've gained a lot of clarity regarding our grandmother. Like us, she made decisions that she would one day come to regret."

Jessica considered her words. "I think I will read them. You finish them and then you can send them back to me. By then I won't be so emotional. Deep down, there's a part of me that really wants to get to know Anabeth. The truth is that I have no right to judge her."

"I feel like I've come full circle here in Mayville.

"I hadn't thought of it that way until you said that," Jessica said, "but you're right. We have come full circle. We started out not knowing anything about our past. Now we actually have history we can draw upon."

Chapter 42

"NATALIA, I'm surprised to see you here," Chrissy said when she walked out of her office. This was her first week back to work after her visit with Jessica. "You're here so often, I'm beginning to wonder if I need to give you a salary."

"Ha. Ha. Very funny," she uttered. "I'm having lunch with my cousin."

"Sabrina's with some clients but she should be done shortly."

"I stopped by here last week. Sabrina said you were on vacation."

"Yes... Aiden and I do that from time to time... go on vacation."

"Where'd you go?"

Chrissy met Natalia's gaze. "Why is that important? It's not like you and I are close friends anymore."

"You have your sister to blame for that. She ruined any chance of us being close."

"Why are you still so focused on Jessica? She left town."

"Where did she go?"

"Like I'd tell you," Chrissy responded. "My sister left so that you'd leave her alone—so that you and she can live your lives in peace."

She returned to her office and shut the door. Chrissy could not understand why Natalia was still so focused on Jessica. Her sister had moved on.

Natalia needed to do the same.

———

"I'M GOING to find out where Jessica is," Natalia muttered.

She questioned Sabrina over lunch. "What's the big secret? She had to file a petition with the court for her probation to be approved to leave North Carolina."

Sabrina took a sip of her tea. "Leave it alone, cuz. Why don't you just enjoy the fact that Jessica's gone. She's not thinking about you—why don't you just return the favor?"

Natalia folded her arms across her chest and settled back against the back of her chair. "She may not be thinking about me, but I will never forget her--she won't get any peace as long as I have breath in my body. Somebody has to make Jessica pay for what she's done. She may have Traynor, Holt and that whole crew brainwashed, but I know what she's really capable of, and I'll never forget."

"You can't live this way," Sabrina said. "It's just not healthy. You might want to take a page out of Jessie Belle's book. This quest for revenge could cost you everything. Is it really worth it? That's what you have to ask yourself."

"What are you talking about? Lose everything?"

"You've told me that you and Dean have been having problems because of this. You don't want to lose your husband behind this."

Chapter 43

NATALIA WAS DETERMINED to have her way in this situation. The following week, she surprised her cousin at home.

"Hey, I wasn't expecting to see you today," Sabrina said. "I thought we were getting together later in the week."

"I was in the area and since I remembered that you were working from home today, I just stopped by—I wasn't interrupting anything, was I?" She was looking for an opportunity to get a look at Sabrina's laptop. Natalia knew she wouldn't be able to do it at the office, so this was her only chance. She had a feeling that what she was looking for, could be found in her cousin's emails.

"No, it's fine. I was about to make some lunch. You hungry?"

"Sure, if it's no bother." Natalia sat down on the sofa. "Hey, do you mind if I use your computer? I need to check my email."

"Go ahead," Sabrina said. "I'm having a turkey sandwich and veggie chips."

"I'll have the same."

Natalia saw that Sabrina's work email was up. She quickly opened up a browser and typed in her web email address. After minimizing the browser, she went through her cousin's email, hoping for some mention of Jessica. She'd been told that the house sold a few days ago.

She found what she was looking for—an email with Jessica's location. Surprised, Natalia whispered, "She's in Mayville, Georgia. I don't believe it."

"Lunch is ready," Sabrina announced.

Natalia took a quick snapshot of the email, then minimized the browser. She closed the one with her work email. "I need to wash my hands and I'll be right there."

You thought you could get away from me, but I've found you. You must have been pretty desperate to move to that hick town, but it doesn't matter where you go—I'm going to ruin your life like you tried to ruin mine.

She strolled into the dining room, grinning.

"What are you so happy about?" Sabrina questioned.

"I just got some great news."

"Congratulations."

"Thank you," Natalia responded as she took a seat. She was pleased with herself over finding Jessica. She had already formulated a plan in her mind.

Sabrina said grace over their simple meal.

"How are things going between you and Noah? You are still seeing him, right?"

"We're good. I'm surprised you remembered his name."

Natalia wiped her mouth with a paper napkin. "Of course, I know his name, Sabrina. You've been dating him for a while now."

"You've never asked about him before."

"I know I've been a bit preoccupied," Natalia said. "I'm sorry. I really do care what's going on in your life. I want you to know that."

Sabrina finished off her sandwich. "It's fine."

"I have to go out of town for a few days, but when I get back—let's plan a girl's trip somewhere. We haven't done that in a long time."

"I'd really like that."

Natalia smiled. "Me, too."

As soon as she returned to the law office, she went straight to Deans office, saying, "Honey, I was asked to speak at John Marshall Law School. I'll need to leave for Atlanta on Thursday and I won't be back until Monday. I have a couple of friends from law school that I want to reconnect with. I hope you won't mind my going."

"That's fine," he responded. "What are you going to talk about?"

"I was thinking of talking about the future of law—building a 21st century practice," Natalia responded, the lie slipping between her lips easily. She actually had a speech prepared on the topic because she'd been invited to speak at the North Carolina Central University School of Law in the Spring. "You think you can handle Minx and

Daniel alone? I can get Sabrina to help out if you need her."

Dean chuckled. "I can handle my own children. I'll just work from home on Thursday and Friday and take Monday off."

She kissed him. "You are such a wonderful husband and father. I'm a very lucky woman."

"Remember that when you get frustrated with me."

"And I need you to remember how much I love you, Dean. I love our life together. Our children—all of you are what's most important to me. Never forget that."

Chapter 44

"THERE'S something you need to know," Sabrina said, rushing into Chrissy's office two days later. "I think Natalia is going after Jessica."

"Why do you say that?"

"I just talked to Dean and he mentioned that Natalia went to Atlanta to speak at a law school, but I'm pretty sure that she lied to him."

"But how does she know where to find Jessica?" Chrissy asked. "Did you tell her?"

"Of course not," Sabrina said. "Natalia came to my house a couple of days ago and while she was there, she asked to use my computer. I believe she went into my emails. I was in the kitchen making lunch and when she joined me—she was acting a bit too pleased with herself. She mentioned that she had to go out of town, but she didn't say where she was going."

"Maybe it's just a coincidence." Chrissy could not

imagine why Natalia would go looking for Jessica. Was she trying to provoke her into doing something that would send her back to prison?

"I don't think so. She told Dean she was speaking at John Marshall Law School. I called and checked —she lied."

"Did you tell her husband?"

Sabrina shook her head no. "I don't want to cause problems between them."

"I can't sit here and let Jessica be ambushed." Chrissy rose to her feet. "I'm going to Mayville. This is a huge weekend for her and Clayton and the last thing they need is Natalia crashing the celebration."

"What are they celebrating?"

"They renovated the church our great-grandfather built. This Sunday is the first service."

"I'm going with you," Sabrina insisted. "Maybe I can talk some sense into Natalia finally. She's gone off the deep end."

Chrissy began pacing. "I know what she's doing. She intends to keep pushing at Jessica until she strikes back. Then she's going to have her sent back to prison."

"Do you think you should warn her?"

"No, because right now, we are speculating. For all we know, Natalia could be cheating on Dean. We don't have any proof of anything. I don't want to stress Jessica out with assumptions. I'm just going to call and let her know that you and I are coming down for the service." Chrissy placed a hand on her growing belly. "I hope we're wrong about Natalia."

They left early Saturday morning.

Once they arrived in Atlanta, Sabrina rented a car and they drove to Mayville.

After checking into the Mayville Inn, she asked Chrissy, "Have you talked to Jessica yet?"

"No, because I know she'd want to know why we're staying at the hotel and not with her. I'll just tell Jessica that we wanted to surprise her when we see her at the church. I did tell my aunt and my father that we were in town, but that I'd see them at the church. I told them not to say a word to Jessica." Chrissy glanced out the window. "Do you think Natalia is staying here or at the Hilton?"

"Natalia is most likely staying in a hotel closer to the law school, just in case Dean calls. I know her. She would give him her hotel and room information because he'd want to have it. It would look suspicious if she's staying this far out."

"If she's really in town, then I'm betting she will be at Mayville Baptist tomorrow for the service," Chrissy announced. "It will provide the perfect stage for her to confront Jessica surrounded by lots of witnesses."

Sabrina sank down on the edge of the queen-sized bed. "I guess it has to come to this, Chrissy. The big showdown."

"You watch too many westerns."

"I love westerns but think about it... even Jessica won't know how much she's changed until she has to face the one person who can bring out the worse in her. As for Natalia, she won't know how much she *needs* to change until she confronts the one person she can't forgive."

Chrissy sat down on the other bed. "You may be right. I just hope that the way this plays out doesn't land my sister back in prison."

"It won't," Sabrina said. "We are going to trust that God is going to show up and work this situation out."

Chapter 45

NATALIA CHECKED her reflection in the full-length mirror. She normally did not like elaborate church hats, but this one looked stunning on her.

She had spent the last three days spying on Jessica and Clayton. On the surface, they were a normal couple who were friendly with the neighbors, but mostly seemed to keep to themselves. From the looks of it, they had completed a lot of work on the two-story house that sat on the lot with the church. Natalia had first seen it when she came down for Jessie Belle's funeral. This updated version was much nicer and more expansive than the original house.

She got in her rental and drove to Mayville. The hour and a half drive from Atlanta was not a bad ride. Traffic was moving steady.

When she pulled into the parking lot of the church, she noticed it was almost full. "All of these people are going to find out who you really are, Jessica," Natalia whispered.

She eased into the sanctuary and found an empty seat halfway toward the front. Natalia kept her face down, pretending to be engrossed in the program she'd been given. She also made a mental list of last minute Christmas gifts she needed to buy. The holiday was a week away.

A wave of guilt washed over Natalia. She should be home with her family, but she convinced herself that coming here was the right thing to do—she couldn't let Jessica pull the wool over the eyes of these innocent people.

Natalia waited until it was time for Clayton to deliver the message. She rose quickly to her feet and stood in the middle of the aisle. "I'm sorry, but I cannot let this farce continue a moment longer. She glared at Jessica, taking momentary pleasure as complete shock siphoned the blood from her face. "There's something you need to know about the man you call a pastor and this woman you call First Lady. While I could find no real proof, I am sure that Clayton Wallace is not the man he's claiming to be—he has no right to be in the pulpit." Natalia looked around. "Where are your bodyguards, Clayton? He used to have at least two with him all the time." She pointed at Jessica. "The main reason I am here is because of his wife. When I met her, her name was *Reina Cannon* and she didn't look like this. She murdered two people, then tried to kill me in my own house, before leaving town and changing her face and her eyes..." Natalia paused for effect. "She had enough work done so that she wouldn't be recognized when she returned to Raleigh. This woman you call *First Lady*, came back to town with a new face and a new name. Jessica Campana. She then tried to frame me for the murders of my friend Charlotte and her husband. This woman even tried to kill her own twin sister before Chrissy had her arrested. Justice was not served when she was sentenced to 16 years and left prison after only eight years. She is evil and should never be allowed to roam free in the world ever again. She most certainly should not be ministering to any of you."

She heard movement behind her. Natalia assumed Clayton had somehow summoned his security team. It didn't matter. She had said what she needed to say.

"Natalia, how could you?"

Surprised, she turned around to face Sabrina and Chrissy. *How did they know I'd be here?* she wondered. *Doesn't matter. The damage has already been done. Jessica is ruined—she'll never be able to hold up her head in this town again.* Natalia glanced over her shoulder to look at Jessica, but to her surprise, she showed no reaction.

"How could you do something like this?" Sabrina asked a second time.

Chrissy's gray eyes slanted in a frown. The tensing of her jaw betrayed her deep frustration.

Nervously, Natalia moistened her lips. "These people needed to know who is living among them. It was the right thing to do."

Chrissy's mouth thinned with displeasure. "I'm going up there to join my sister and brother-in-law."

"We all have to do what we have to do," Natalia

responded. "We have to be very careful of who we allow to lead us," she added loudly. Deep down, she was puzzled that people were still seated all around her, just staring from her to Jessica—their gazes darting back and forth. *Why weren't they leaving?* "She's psychotic and out of control."

Jessica's voice pierced the silence. "Everything the woman said was true."

Chapter 46

JESSICA KEPT her expression bland when a few people got up to leave. To her amazement, the rest remained in the sanctuary. They were either eager to see how this would all unfold, so that they would have something to gossip about for the rest of the week, or they were staying in support of her and Clayton. It was too soon to know which.

Chrissy joined them in the pulpit. They stood together, facing the congregation.

"Everything this woman said is true," she repeated. "I do not deny any of it, but I am not that same woman who went to prison for her crimes. However, Natalia is wrong in her accusations that I am psychotic and out of control."

The air in the sanctuary crackled with energy, and the voices of people seated in the congregation created a dull but rising roar.

"Let her speak," one of the men seated near the front shouted.

It should've come to a grinding halt. But instead, the

roar only lowered to a loud hum.

When Jessica picked up the microphone, silence enveloped the room.

"I do not deny or dismiss my past, but I will not allow it to define me or dismantle my ministry. Those of you who have gotten to know my husband—he has been forthcoming about his past—not as a source of pride, but as a testimony to the transforming power of Christ Jesus. While in prison, I repented of my sins and asked God's forgiveness. Just like everyone else who believes, our record of sins was wiped clean at the cross—God no longer sees our past. From that moment forward, I have worked daily to serve my heavenly Father. I want people to see that if God did such an amazing work in my life, then they can be confident that He will do the same for them."

Clayton wrapped an arm around her. "What my wife didn't tell you was that she suffered from years of physical and verbal abuse by her adopted parents. She also had a mental disorder which had gone undiagnosed for years until after she was arrested. She has since started treatment and is doing well. Our intent was never to deceive anyone. We wanted all of you to get to know the woman she is today—she would have shared her truth with you. If any of you have any questions or concerns, present them to us now. Natalia was right when she said that you have to be careful about who you choose to be your pastor. I personally believe a pastor who has been caught in immorality, extortion and such should be brought before the Church, disciplined according to the Scriptures, and be unable to move to another place. I believe God will hold a local congregation accountable for not dealing with that situation, especially if they allow him to move on without warning the next congregation. Some of you know Pastor Traynor Deveraux and he gave us this church. He ordained me—those who know him, knows that he would not have done so if he felt I was not ready."

Several people in the congregation nodded in agreement.

"I said all that to say this: there is an enormous difference between dealing with an ungodly pastor and a true man of God. I ask that you all pray for wisdom and discernment. If my wife and I have to minister to an empty church—we will do so. Today will not stop us from following the call placed on our hearts by God. I am going to do His will and trust Him to fill the congregation. Mayville has become our home and we have no intentions of leaving."

Chrissy took the microphone from Clayton. "Good morning, my name is Chrissy St. Paul. I am a minister at Bright Hope Christian Church under the leadership of Pastor Traynor Deveraux. Jessica is my twin sister—we were separated at birth and because of it, we both had to deal with some very bad things growing up. We both made some bad choices because we believed that there was a seed of righteousness in our anger. I know everyone in this sanctuary can relate because none of us are perfect."

She paused a moment, then continued. "Natalia called my sister psychotic—she talked about her being out of control. None of us deny that she was once a woman filled with rage. The old Jessica—this building would have been in disarray by now, but praise God, she is a different person now. That rage is gone. The Bible tells us that rage is a disposition toward sin. Proverbs 29: 22 tells us that *one given to anger causes much transgression*. One thing you have to understand is that our moment of rage is not about the person who has shamed us—it's about whether we will allow ourselves to stoop to shameful levels in order to defend shame. When Jessica was in prison, my sister told me something that has stayed with me. She said she was prepared for the judgement that would come when she was released—she told me that God was already preparing her heart for that day. He'd told her that when people judge or label you, bracket the offense for just a moment. She said the Lord told her that it's not about the offense. It's about you. It's about getting a handle on your soul, because if you can't—you'll stumble headlong into shame in ways your accusers will be happy to exploit. We implore you to search what God would have you do in this situation. I am proud of Clayton and Jessica and I know that they mean what they say—they will come into this building every Sunday and preach themselves happy—just the two of them, because of the faith they have in God."

Jessica closed her eyes and began to sing.

> *"Amazing Grace, How sweet the sound that*
> *saved a wretch like me. I once was lost,*
> *but now am found t'was blind but now*
> *I see...*

Clayton and Chrissy joined her, followed by the choir.

Chapter 47

"I GUESS this didn't go quite the way you'd planned," Chrissy said to Natalia. They were standing in the back of the empty church. "What the enemy meant for bad—God turned it around. Instead of making my sister look bad— you made yourself look like the bitter woman you are. You should be ashamed of yourself."

Natalia set her chin in a stubborn line. "Your sister is the one who should be shamed," she argued. "She got off much too easy."

"You really think that?" Jessica asked from behind her. "Well, I didn't. In that stifling prison cell that was my home for eight years, the dead came knocking... like noises beneath the floor... harassing, insistent, hate-filled, and bitter sounds all night long. Sleep just wouldn't come most nights. Even now, I still have trouble sleeping some nights."

Natalia turned to face Jessica. "Am I supposed to feel sorry for you?"

"No, I don't expect you to feel anything for me. I made

your life miserable. I just want you to know that I'm still paying the price for my actions. It didn't stop when I walked out of that prison. The thing is that while I was able to leave mine—you are still in your prison."

Frowning, Natalia asked, "What prison?"

"The one made of hate," Jessica said.

"The farthest you can get from our heavenly Father is hate, Natalia," Chrissy interjected. "Hate is a destructive force that can hurt you more than you hate my sister. Trust me, I know this to be true. Hate is sin. It keeps you in bondage. Jesus came to set us free from all sin and all that hurts our relationship with the Father. God has a path for us to take to win in life and enjoy life. Hate will not take us there, but love will."

"What you did to me... to my friends..."

Jessica's eyes filled with tears. "I'm so very sorry, Natalia. I can't change what happened. All I'm trying to do is try and keep someone else from making that same mistake. Living with what I've done is not easy. I think of them all the time. When I went away, I asked Clayton to set up a fund for Charlotte's daughter. She will never want for anything financially. I couldn't give her back her parents, but I wanted to do something."

Natalia did not respond.

"I am truly sorry, and I hope that one day you will be able to forgive me."

"You might not want to hold your breath waiting on that to happen. I'm just saying."

Jessica wiped her face. "There is nothing else I can say. I've done my part."

Chapter 48

"YOU REALLY NEED to let this go. Give it to God," Sabrina stated when she walked outside with Natalia. "The Bible tells us to cast our cares upon Him, because He cares for us. Bitterness will eat you up and you'll be a slave to Jessica."

"Do you think I like the person I've become?" Natalia shook her head. "Jessica did this to me and I'm sorry, but I can't forgive her."

"Forgiveness is the first step to healing the hurt she's caused."

"Sabrina, I hear this enough from Dean. I don't need to hear it from you, too. Nobody seems to care about the way I'm feeling. You don't understand what she put me through."

"I do understand, Natalia. More than you know."

She regarded Sabrina with somber curiosity. "What do you mean?"

"I was attacked one night by a john. After that incident, I was afraid all the time and I knew that I could not stay in that life. I had two choices—to either give in to fear and anger, embrace victimization and be a lesser version of myself; or choose to have hope and trust in a power that was greater than my own. It was in that moment that I made a decision that would give me the peace I needed. After the attack, he was arrested on some parole violation. I went to visit him while he was in jail. I confronted him—not to antagonize him, but to forgive him, Natalia. It was only then that I was able to take back my power. When I walked out of that place, I was no longer afraid of him."

"How were you able to do it?"

"My reliance on the Lord enabled me to dig deep to find not only forgiveness, but also healing, Natalia. The actual process of getting past the trauma... for me, meant a full surrender to God."

"I never knew about that."

"We weren't on speaking terms when it happened," Sabrina said with a slight shrug. "It was when you wanted nothing to do with me because I was in the *life*."

"Was I really that awful to you?"

"Yes, you were, Natalia."

Sabrina's response hammered at her. "I'm sorry. I don't think I've ever really apologized to you."

"I'm not the person I used to be. You're not the self-absorbed mean girl anymore. You changed. People *can* change."

"I lied to Dean."

"He'll forgive you because he loves you."

Natalia glanced over her shoulder toward the church. A flash of genuine regret ripped through her. "I never should've come here."

"No, you shouldn't have," Sabrina agreed. "It's not up to you to judge Jessica and Clayton. Go home to Dean and your adorable children."

Natalia nodded. "Are you flying back with Chrissy?"

"The three of us can go together. I'll make the reservations."

Chrissy walked over to where they were standing. "We need to head to the airport."

"Natalia's going to fly back with us," Sabrina announced.

"That's good."

"Congratulations, Chrissy. I just realized that I never told you that."

"Thank you. Aiden and I are thrilled."

"I loved both my pregnancies."

"At my age, this is likely to be my only one, but it's fine because I'm having twins."

A genuine smile lit Natalia's face. "That's wonderful. I've always wanted to have a set of twins. Make sure you're getting your proper rest."

"I try because I tire so easily these days."

"That's normal."

The three women talked about pregnancy and childbirth all the way to the airport and on the flight home.

"Chrissy, for the record," Natalia said when they landed at RDU, "I don't feel good about what I did earlier. I didn't apologize to Jessica, but I am sorry."

"I'll let her know."

"Minx has been wanting to see Lenore. Maybe we can get the girls together one weekend."

Chrissy smiled. "Lenore and I both would like that, Natalia."

Chapter 49

"NOW THAT YOU know the ugly truth, I was sure you never wanted to see me again," Jessica told her father when he came by the house later that evening. She had planned to tell him everything, but Natalia had to show up and try to ruin her life. She was pretty sure her biological father did not want someone like her in his family. Strangely, Jessica was okay with it. She was grateful for the time she had been able to spend with him. "I wasn't going to keep this from you—I just wanted the chance for you to get to know the person I am now."

"I wish I had stayed around to be a father to you. I'm so sorry."

"Jessie Belle's mother used to say that we can't live in yesterday. Well, she is right about that. I can choose to drown in my past or I can ride the tide to the future. I accepted my responsibility for all the wrong I've done, and I paid for it in prison. Now, I'd just like to move forward."

"I want you to know that I'm very proud to be your father. I want you to meet the rest of your family."

Stunned, Jessica stared at him.

"I've told my wife everything and she's looking forward to getting to know you. So are your brothers, Jett and Jenson."

"They may change their mind when they find out I was in prison for murder."

"I don't believe they will," Brockton said. "Jenson's been in trouble a few times. The last time landed him in prison for four years. He came home a changed man. Going to prison saved his life—that's what his mother and I believe. It will do him good to meet you and Clayton. He feels like no one really understands what he's been through."

"I don't think anyone who hasn't been in prison *can* truly understand," Jessica responded. "I would love to meet your family."

"The Jessie Belle that I knew... she wasn't a bad person. She just wanted her way in everything."

"That never changed," she uttered. "She was hungry for power."

"I can't help but wonder how your life would've differed if Jessie Belle and I had run off together."

"It doesn't do us any good to think that way." Jessica shrugged in resignation. "This is our reality."

"I suppose you're right."

"You have no idea how much it means that I have this opportunity to get to know you, Brockton. I'm content and happy." She reached over and covered his hand with her own. "Everything's great in my life. Chrissy is happily married with two children and a set of twins on the way. I don't want you to have any regrets. We're good."

"You're not just saying this because you don't want to hurt my feelings?"

Jessica smiled. "I'm telling you the truth."

"I know that you don't need a daddy, but…"

She cut him off by saying, "You will always be my father, Brockton."

Jessica walked him to the front door.

"That woman…"

"Natalia," she said.

"When she started talking—the person she described… that's not the beautiful and intelligent woman standing beside me. That person she was talking about doesn't exist anymore."

Jessica embraced her father. "Thank you."

"I'll be leaving in the morning."

"Travel safe," she told him.

"If you have some time, we can talk later in the week," Brockton said. "I'll give you a call."

"I'd like that," she responded. "Wednesday or Thursday works best for me."

They embraced a second time.

"Your dad's gone?" Clayton inquired when Jessica entered the bedroom.

She nodded. "He left a few minutes ago. We had a great talk."

"Today could have turned out differently," he said

when they settled in the family room. "I know I wanted to jump down there and toss Natalia out the church."

"That's what she wanted us to do. She came looking for a fight and I was ready to give her one, but then God spoke to me. He reminded me of the day I gave my life to Him. He reminded me that I promised to leave Natalia to Him."

Clayton shook his head. "That woman is letting hate eat her up."

"That's what makes me sad. "You and I both have been in her shoes. We know what it can do to a person. Although I never really cared for Natalia, I always thought she had it together, for the most part." Jessica looked at her husband. "Promise me you're not going to let her slide. No complaints with the Bar Association, no lawsuits. Just leave her alone."

"It's harassment, babe. What if she comes back?"

"I don't think she will," Jessica said. "I could be wrong because she hates me, but I just don't think she'll be back—she has nothing to gain." She took Clayton's hand. "Bae, let's pray. I feel in my spirit that we need to pray for Natalia."

Chapter 50

"HEY HONEY," Natalia greeted Dean when she entered the house.

"Did you get the satisfaction you so desperately needed" Dean asked, his tone cool and aloof. "I know you went to Georgia after Jessica. I hope it was worth it." She didn't bother to ask how he knew—it didn't really matter anymore.

"I'm sorry for lying, but you really didn't give me any choice," she stated. "You seem to be on her side."

"I'm on the side of what's right. That woman has served her time and is trying to start over in another *state*. She's not bothering you."

"They have a church. Can you believe she's trying to minister to people? Her and that thug of a husband."

"What business is it of yours?"

Natalia folded her arms across her chest. "I felt the members should know the truth about them."

"And I'm sure you told them." There was an edge to his voice.

"I sure did," Natalia confessed.

"Did they all just get up and leave after you vilified Jessica and her husband?"

She shook her head no. "A couple of people left, but that was about it. The church was filled to capacity, although it wasn't all that big to start with."

Dean surveyed her face. "So, do you feel better now?"

Natalia shook her head. "Not really."

"So, what's next on your quest for revenge?"

"Dean..."

"Have you considered that this is exactly what made Jessica the person she became—she was out for revenge."

"Are you actually comparing me to her?"

"You think about that," Dean responded. "You also need to think about something else. You weren't always the person you are now. People *can* change."

Natalia met his gaze. "I know that some people are capable of change, but—"

"We're going around in circles," Dean interjected. "Frankly, I'm tired of this discussion. It's getting us nowhere. I have some work to do, so I'll be in the office."

He left before she could utter a response.

Natalia went in search of her children. She had missed them and right now she needed to feel their arms around her.

Minx and Daniel were in the bonus room playing.

"Mommy," they shouted in unison.

"I missed my babies," she said, hugging them both.

After watching a movie with them, Natalia went down to check on Dean. He was still in his office.

"Are you still angry with me?"

"I'm not angry with you, Natalia. Just disappointed."

"Dean, I really wish I could just forget everything, but I can't."

"I don't want to keep talking about this—it's getting us nowhere."

"Look at what Jessica's doing to us. We're fighting because of her."

Dean shook his head. *"You're doing this to us*, Natalia. You are so focused on ruining Jessica's life..." He released a sigh of resignation. "I just want us to move on."

"I want to move on, too. I just don't know how." Natalia began to cry. "I can't forget how she tried to kill me —I don't want her to ever forget it either."

Dean embraced her. "I really think you need to see someone."

Natalia nodded. "I think so, too."

"The more I think about it, I really believe that anger sometimes is a way to ward off feelings of powerlessness," he stated. "There is research which suggests that our brain secretes analgesic-like norepinephrine when we're provoked—well, it also produces the amphetamine-like hormone epinephrine, which enables us to experience a surge of energy throughout our body."

"So, you're saying that all this anger I'm feeling is like an adrenaline rush."

Dean nodded. "Think about it. A person or situation somehow makes us feel defeated or powerless—those hormones are capable of transforming these helpless feelings into anger which provides a heightened sense of control."

"My anger makes me feel powerful and less of a victim—that's what you're saying."

"You may want to consider it."

"I don't want to be scared all the time, Dean. I can't live that way anymore."

"I told you that I won't let anyone hurt you, sweetheart. I mean it. I'll protect you and our children with my life."

"I feel the same way," Natalia said.

"Jessica is out of our lives for good. Let's leave her in Georgia."

"Maybe I shouldn't have gone down there—now I've given her a reason to come gunning for me."

"You said she apologized to you once again."

Natalia nodded. "She did. I just don't know if I can believe her."

"Think about it, the woman you once knew wouldn't have let you leave Georgia, if she really wanted to hurt you."

"You're probably right." She released a long sigh. "Jessica looked me straight in my eyes when she asked me to forgive her."

"What did you see in the depths?"

"Repentance," Natalia said. "I can't believe that I'm saying this, but it's the truth. She looked like someone who was deeply sorry for her actions. I didn't see anger... just sorrow."

"Yet, you can't forgive her?"

"I can't," Natalia confessed. She covered her face with trembling hands. "I'm sorry, but I can't do it."

Chapter 51

THE NEXT MORNING, Jessica was up early and at the grocery store. She felt a twinge of apprehension when she glimpsed one of the women who was present when Natalia went on her diatribe. She hoped to ease by Clara Blaylock unnoticed.

"First Lady, I'm so glad I ran into you."

"Good morning, Sister Clara."

"I want you to know that your testimony up there... my son is in prison... this gives me hope. He recently got baptized and told me that he'd given his life to the Lord. I didn't believe him, but now I see that people can really change." Clara's eyes filled with tears. "This is an answer to my prayers. I thank the Lord for you and Pastor Clayton."

Jessica pulled a tissue out of her purse and handed it to Clara. "Give your son a chance. Believe in him until he gives you a reason not to," she said.

"First Lady, I applaud your courage and that young

woman—she in my prayers 'cause she done let all that anger take root in her heart. I'm so glad the man that my boy hurt done forgave him. He told him so right there in the courtroom."

"That's all I want from Natalia, but it's not something she can do right now."

"Well, don't let it stop you from doing what God has called you to do. And don't you hide your head in shame. The people that came to that church yesterday—did so because some of us knew your granddaddy. Rev. Holt baptized me, and he married me and my late husband. He was a good man. I loved that church and I was so happy when y'all came and renovated it. We could tell that you and Pastor Clayton good folk. Small town like this... somebody always watching. We ain't seen nothing but good works coming from you and your husband. The folk that walked out—they ain't s'posed to be there no way."

"Sister Clara, thank you so much for encouraging me. I hope you'll come to the Women's Ministry Tea on Saturday."

"Oh, I'll be there. If you like, I'll bring a lemon pound cake. Everybody says I make the best in this town."

"Then you should bring one if it's not too much trouble," Jessica said. "I love lemon pound cake."

"I'll make one just for you, First Lady."

From the time she met Clara, she had been trying to get her to drop the *First Lady* label, but it was too no avail, so Jessica gave up. "Thank you, Sister Clara. You have truly blessed me this morning."

Clayton was reading the Bible when she returned

home. She put the groceries away, then walked into the sunroom to join him.

He closed it and placed it on a side table when she sat down beside him. "I spent this morning with the Lord. I wanted to make sure I was doing what He'd called me to do... you know... the ministry. I don't want to be out of His will."

She gave him a sidelong look. "Why are you second guessing yourself?"

"Have you ever wondered whether our past disqualifies us from ministry? When Natalia was reciting our sins to the congregation, I felt like I was unqualified to preach the gospel. I even heard in my spirit that I was too polluted to preach."

"You know that was the enemy talking—it wasn't God."

"I know that, but for some reason 1 Chronicles 28:3 kept coming back to me. In that scripture, David is called a *man of bloodshed*, reminding me that I was an unholy criminal. The force of those words on my soul, Jess... they haunted me... condemned me. I called Traynor not too long ago because I needed to talk this through."

"What did he tell you?"

"In simple terms, he basically said I was being an idiot. When Traynor started mentoring me, one of the first things he told me was that the sins of our pasts preach to us, which will cause us to question whether we're fit to step into a pulpit."

"Paul is my person I think of whenever I feel that way," Jessica said. "I think of the way God rescued him from his sins. The thing I like most about Paul is that he never once forgot who he was. He didn't try to bury it."

Clayton nodded in agreement. "Paul shares his story two different times in the book of Acts. In fact, he often led with his testimony. He was able to see his past in such a way that it did not condemn or destroy him. He didn't allow the past to send him down a path of self-accusation."

"Exactly," Jessica interjected. "Paul found that the bitterness of his past made Christ sweeter to him."

"Babe, that will preach right there. People need to see their past life through the same gospel lens as Paul. I was once this, but in Christ, I am now *this!*"

"Praise God," Jessica murmured as tears welled in her eyes as inexplicable joy filled her soul. "Thank you, Jesus. Because of You, my sinful past has been transformed from being the source of my identity to be the source of my testimony."

"Hallelujah," Clayton said, raising his hand toward heaven.

Epilogue

5 Years Later

"I STILL CAN'T BELIEVE how much the church has grown," Jessica said. "We started with fifty-four members and now we have over two hundred. We've got members coming from as far as Bellhaven." They were in the office going over the plans for the day. She wanted everything to go smoothly.

Clayton placed a gentle kiss on her forehead. "This is the first Sunday in the new building. I'm so glad Eric was able to come from Savannah. That young man is on fire for the Lord."

"I can't wait to hear his message. Does he know that you're going to offer him a position as youth pastor?" Eric Chastain had just graduated from seminary. Clayton, Holt and Traynor all attended his graduation at his invitation. Her husband really believed in the young man and had agreed to mentor him.

Jessica heard laughter. "I'd better go check on the children."

Holt, Frankie, Aiden, and Chrissy all stayed with Traynor at the house in Brookhaven. She and Clayton gave their parents a night off. Seven nieces and nephews were a lot to keep up with, but the older ones were an immense help to her.

She found Holt Jr. and Caleb in the kitchen making waffles and scrambled eggs. "You guys are great," Jessica told them. "There's some fresh fruit in the fridge we can have for breakfast as well."

"Where's Uncle Clay?" Caleb inquired.

Jessica nodded. "He'll be here shortly. He loves waffles."

"I know," Caleb responded. "He and I like to eat them with strawberries on top and whip cream."

"That's right." She gestured toward the stairs. "Are the girls still upstairs?"

"Holt Jr. nodded. "You know how girls are... they take all day to get dressed if you let them."

"Lenore's ready," Caleb said. "She was combing Bella's hair when I came down here." Bella and Brian were Chrissy and Aiden's miracle babies. Jessica could hardly believe they were going to start kindergarten in the Fall.

"Where's Brian?"

"I'm over here." The voice came from the family room. Brian was dressed and sitting in the overstuffed chair facing the television. "When we gonna eat?"

"Soon," Jessica responded. "C'mon over to the table, sweetie."

"Auntie, why are you always smiling?" he asked. "Is it because God loves you?"

She fingered the sandy brown curls on the five-year old boy's head. "That's exactly why I smile, baby."

"I love you."

"That makes me smile, too." Jessica bent down and kissed his cheek. "I love me some you, sweetie pie."

He giggled.

Clayton joined Brian at the table. "Are you stealing my sugar again?"

"She's my auntie and I love her."

"She's my wife," he countered. "And I adore her."

"No fighting," Jessica teased. "There's enough of me to go around."

Determined to have the last word, Brian muttered, "Auntie loves me more."

She chuckled, then said, "I'm going to check on the girls."

Ten minutes later, everyone was seated around the dining room table talking and laughing as they ate breakfast.

Jessica eye's teared up at the scene unfolding around her. She was blessed beyond measure—the mere thought was humbling. Clayton was now Senior Pastor and had two assistant pastors serving under him. Jessica felt she could better serve her husband by heading the women's ministry. She was past the halfway mark in obtaining a degree in Psychology, with a concentration in counseling.

They met the rest of the family at the church. Jessica was thrilled that all her family had come to show their support, including Brockton, his wife, her brothers, and their families. For her, life just could not get any better. After greeting everyone, she and Clayton navigated to the administrative offices. Along with the new sanctuary, the new building also housed the Grainger-Holt Youth Center, bringing Clayton's dream of helping teenagers to fruition.

The night Anabeth Grainger Holt took Jessie Belle to Gloria Ricks, she had no idea what she'd put in motion. She did not know the plans God had for my sister and me.

Jessie raised her eyes heavenward. *Thank you, Father for allowing me to live. That night could've ended differently, but You had a plan. Everything that happened in my life—You designed the path for my purpose and I thank You. I give you glory for sticking with me when I didn't even know You were there.*

Tears filled her eyes. *When I... Lord, when I took lives... when I broke Your heart with my sins... Lord, You stayed with me. I thank You, Lord, for loving me through my worse self. I am so grateful.*

She felt Clayton's arms around her. "It's almost time for service to begin."

Jessica glanced at her reflection in a nearby mirror, then planted a kiss on his lips. "I'm ready."

Book Club Discussion Guide

---

1. In the Bible, there was no redemption for Queen Jezebel. Compare Jessica's life with that of Jezebel. How were they similar? How were they different?

2. Jessie Belle denied her daughters, but their biological father accepted them with open arms and without question. Do you think it would have made a difference in the lives of Chrissy and Jessica? Explain your response.

3. Discuss the difference between judging the actions of others and judging their motives. Do we have the right to judge anyone other than ourselves?

4. Could you relate to any of the characters in this series? Please explain your response.

- Jessica
- Jessie Belle

- Natalia
- Chrissy
- Sabrina
- Anabeth
- Traynor
- Aiden
- Clayton
- Dean

5. Natalia found herself unable to forgive Jessica. Have you ever been in a situation where forgiveness would not come? How did you handle it?

6. Jessica and Clayton both chose to accept God's love and forgiveness. They were so sick of their own sins, that they repeated and turned their lives around. However, there are people who believe that some sins, such as murder are not redeemable. Society often treats ex-cons as lifetime criminals—even those who are diligently trying to prove they deserve a second chance. Share your thoughts on this topic.

7. In 1 & 2 Kings, Queen Jezebel's offspring imbibed and continued the wickedness they grew up in. Jezebel's evil influence was revived in her daughter Athaliah of Judea. Her malign character reappears in her eldest son, Ahaziah, who, like his idolatrous mother, was a devout worshiper of Baal. Her second son, Jehoram was another image of his mother—further corrupt fruit from a corrupt tree. What are your thoughts on generational curses? What can we do today to break cycles like these?

Jezebel Series

Jezebel

Jezebel's Daughter

Jezebel's Revenge

Jezebel: The Prequel